THE ARRANGED BREAKUP

A JOURNEY OF LOVE AND LOSS

PRIYANKA SINGH

Contents

Acknowledgment

I am deeply grateful to my husband (Mayank) for his unwavering support and encouragement throughout this journey. I also want to thank my sister-in-law (Biswamugdha) for taking time out of her busy schedule and reading the draft multiple times.

To my family, for their endless love and belief in me, and to my lovely daughter (Mridali) for her excitement and joy in holding a book authored by her mother. Their faith in me has been my greatest strength.

A big thank you to my readers for taking the time to read this book. Your support and enthusiasm are precious gifts to me. I hope this book brings you joy and insight, as it did for me while writing it.

1
The Run

It was a hot and sunny day. Dry and gusty wind was blowing, and leaves were rustling on the deserted street. The houses on both sides of the lane seemed abandoned. It was the usual summer noon, when people do not dare to step out. The noisy air cooler in the room was disturbing Kashvi. The somber mood had again taken her into its custody, and she found it difficult to breathe in the room. The sound of the noisy air cooler was hitting her too hard, causing excruciating pain in her head. She opened the casement to breathe in some fresh air and felt a warm puff on her face; it was scorching hot. Though it was a sultry noon, she decided to step out to get rid of this gloomy feeling.

People on the roads seemed to be exhausted because of the hot day. Hawkers sitting on the side of the road were wiping their sweat. Children returning from school looked fagged. As she was frazzled, everything seemed dull and exhausting to her.

She was walking briskly to run away from the bitter thoughts that were tormenting her. She was sweating profusely, and the perspiration was making her hair wet. Due to the sun's heat, her face had turned red; beads of sweat rolled down from her forehead and found their way behind her ears. The dupatta around her neck was dampened, and its edges rolled up, covering her arms, which had also become wet from her sweat.

After walking for a while, she reached the area near a temple. She wanted to go and sit inside, but the temple was closed. The marble steps of the temple were covered with sand grains, and the steps appeared yellowish instead of white. Taking off her slippers, she sat down on the step, which appeared cleaner and brighter than the rest. The sun was shining at its peak, and it was hard to open eyes in such brightness.

Two earthen pots, each wrapped with linen cloth, were kept inside a slight shade next to the temple. She paced herself to the shade. A small, metal ladle-shaped vessel hung on the side of the pot. She held the string and removed the plates, which were placed on top of the pot.

She did a brief inspection of the water, then dropped the ladle into the pot to draw some water, forming a cup with one hand to hold it. She splashed water on her face, and it made her feel. After gaining her normal breath, she looked around to distract herself from the haunting thoughts. In that muggy hour, the only respite was an ice-cream seller passing out cones to the schoolchildren.

Unexpectedly, she heard someone calling her name. The voice was coming from an autorickshaw that was stationed near a hawker in the vicinity of the temple. When she set her eyes on the autorickshaw, she saw a girl waving at her as she stepped outside.

"Come, what are you doing here? You will fall sick. Don't you know it is a heatwave this summer? And the temple only opens at four in the evening. You can never keep track of time." The girl projected her voice—it was Sarika, Kashvi's best friend.

Kashvi stumbled while wearing her slippers and walked toward the autorickshaw.

"Come fast," Sarika held her hand and dragged her inside the autorickshaw.

"It is so hot, and you chose this place to hang out. Have you gone mad? Look at your face, it looks so dull." Sarika immediately cut short her statement, looking at Kashvi's reaction to her last statement.

"I am talking to my friend. Stop glaring at us in the mirror, look ahead, and drive carefully," she commented to the auto driver, looking at the rearview mirror.

There was silence for a few seconds. Sarika slowly rolled her eyes to watch Kashvi's expression. She still looked agitated, so Sarika started directing the auto driver again to ease the heaviness.

"Take the straight road, and when you see a provision store on the right side of the road, take an immediate turn from there. You can slow down on that street; there are a lot of speed breakers on the way. Don't drive rashly. Keep in mind that if the ride is jerky, I will deduct ten rupees."

Hearing that, the driver applied the brakes knowingly. Sarika waved from left to right inside the autorickshaw and bumped her shoulder against Kashvi's. The driver started the autorickshaw again and turned up the loud music. He was driving fast; Kashvi and Sarika were holding onto the side rods, swaying with the sudden turns and brakes. As the autorickshaw entered the lane next to the provision store, Kashvi asked the driver to slow down and stop after a few meters, near the house with a tree in front of it.

"Why do you play such loud music?" she asked the driver.

"With this loud music and these unnecessary decorations hanging and swaying inside your auto, I felt like I had joined some procession. And who charges so much for eight kilometers?"

Kashvi was waiting on the porch, watching Sarika argue with the driver. It had been more than five minutes now. The sultry noon was making it difficult to stand even on the porch. Still, it looked like Sarika had forgotten about the heatwave forecast. Kashvi was aware of her voluble nature and knew this prattle wouldn't end without an intervention.

"Can you come inside now?" Kashvi asked. There was a deliberate stress, a pause between each word.

"You people never go by the meter, and on top of that, so much arrogance." She overheard Kashvi.

"Madam, this is how royal rides are charged," the driver replied with a smirk, as he returned the change.

"Your conversations never end," Kashvi said as she went inside her house. While Sarika was still arguing with the driver, Kashvi's mother, Mrs. Sharma, came outside and called her in an astonishingly ungracious manner; her single call was enough to summon Sarika inside the house.

The driver, too, accelerated as fast as he could after hearing Mrs. Sharma's call.

"Namaste, aunty!" she greeted Kashvi's mother.

Kashvi and her mother lived on the first floor, and the ground floor was vacant and available for rent. It was rarely occupied by tenants because of Kashvi's skeptical approach toward everyone.

"On this boiling day, you should serve something cold and refreshing to drink." Mrs. Sharma pinned her gaze on Sarika as she climbed the stairs.

"I mean, cold water with ice cubes would also be good." Sarika fumbled.

They entered the living room; Mrs. Sharma went into the kitchen. Sarika jumped and sat on the sofa next to Kashvi. Kashvi moved slightly to give her some space. Sarika pulled the cushion and hugged it tightly.

"Tell me, what have you decided?" Sarika asked.

"Give me some time, don't start immediately. Can we talk about something else?" replied Kashvi irritably.

"Yes, of course, I can talk about anything; it is you who needs to decide what that 'something else' is," Sarika chuckled.

Mrs. Sharma entered the room with three glasses of chilled juice; each topped with two floating ice cubes. She placed the tray on the coffee table. Dewdrops on the outer surface of the glasses were making the tray wet. Kashvi passed it to Sarika, wiping the base of the glass. Mrs. Sharma joined their conversation and remarked, "The problem lies here."

"No, aunty." Sarika hesitated as she checked the glass to prevent the cushion from getting wet.

"It is not about the juice glass; I am talking about Kashvi." Mrs. Sharma raised her eyebrows.

"You don't dare to face reality and never want to talk about important things. It is a moot point that will never make your life easier," she ended, looking at Kashvi.

To change the subject, Sarika quickly passed the other glass to Mrs. Sharma and pressed her own glass over her face. "Oh, it feels so good."

Mrs. Sharma continued, "You don't want to accept the truth. Learn to face reality and stop running away from it. If I had been in your place, I would have..."

Before her mother could complete her sentence, Kashvi interjected, "No, nobody is in my place, and that is why it is easy for all of you to talk rubbish."

"I pray that nobody should be in my place. Why does someone have to face…" Mrs. Sharma took her glass and left the room in anger, leaving the bitter dissension half-heard.

"I am not a coward, but I somehow don't feel like talking about anything right now," Kashvi replied in a low tone.

Sarika could sense the grief in her voice. She drank the juice to the dregs and placed her glass on the tray. While thinking of ways to cheer up her dear friend, she asked Kashvi to form rings on the table using the wet base of the glass. They formed a few, and the table looked shabby with those spots.

"It has been months now; you should move on," Sarika suggested, holding the brim and covering the ring that formed as the juice drops dried on the tray.

"Look at those rings; they have faded. The power of nature to diminish gradually," Sarika added with a subtle intensity, and stared at her friend.

Memories and experiences are part of life, and everything fades away with time. Kashvi comprehended Sarika's intention.

After chatting for a while, they both went out shopping. The narrow lane of the market was packed; one could only see heads and shoulders rubbing against each other. They hopped from shop to shop and bought beautiful embroidered cotton kurtas, gorgeous phulkari dupattas, designer mojaris, metal bangles clinking like a chandelier, and dazzling earrings. Carrying heavy bags, they both stopped at a lassi shop. The place looked crowded, but they managed to find a table near a fan.

In a few minutes, creamy frothy glasses were served at the table. The dry fruits sprinkled on the lassi made it more flavorsome. They both drank the lassi and talked heartily at the table.

"Don't you think shopping is meditation for girls? Girls don't need meditation classes. You take them to a crowded market, where you get everything at a lower price and watch them regain their energy. On top of that, winning a deal with shopkeepers to reduce the price from 1000 to 300 is like an extra spiritual session."

"You are a Gyani baba, Sarika. Walk fast, it is already late; let us go back home."

It was getting darker, and with the sunset, the cool breeze had begun to blow. They got into a shared autorickshaw and settled in with their heavy shopping bags. Sarika handed some of her bags to a lady sitting next to her, which was indeed an unsolicited help. The lady looked annoyed with the heavy bags on her lap, and Sarika turned a blind eye and kept talking some nonsense until they reached their place. While Kashvi handed change to the driver, Sarika snatched the bags back and asked the driver to drop that lady carefully.

"Aunty, you look tired after this long and bumpy ride."

The lady looked even angrier, and before she could open her mouth, Sarika continued, "Don't worry, aunty, he will drop you safely."

Kashvi dragged her by the elbow, "Can we go?" she snapped.

Giggling and chattering, they entered the living room. Mrs. Sharma smiled at them and asked them to get ready and have dinner. After the scrumptious dinner, they both ran into the room to check the stuff they had brought from shopping. They tried everything to see whether it fits in.

They heard Mrs. Sharma announcing from another room. "I am going to sleep now; I have to get up early tomorrow." They both decided to go to the terrace.

Kashvi spread the mat, and Sarika threw the pillows on it. For hours, they kept staring at the sky, filled with stars, twinkling and glittering, forming beautiful patterns. They experienced peace and calm gazing at the sky, full of sparkling spots. There was a profound silence.

"We trouble ourselves so much in our daily life, whereas one day we will all be lost in this huge universe," Kashvi uttered with a heavy voice.

With a deep breath, Sarika replied, "Hmm, I think I was wrong. One can even come to your terrace to find peace instead of shopping."

Kashvi wanted to laugh, but something held her back, and she smiled.

Sarika looked at her best friend's face and caught a flicker of emotion in her eyes.

"I don't want you to see you living like some tragedy queen. You have to forget everything and move on." "Waiting and thinking about someone unworthy is not just a waste of time, but you are also hurting your loved ones and yourself."

"I am not waiting for anyone," Kashvi replied firmly. They spent a few hours on the terrace talking about the past.

Like most parents, Mrs. Sharma was not asleep and couldn't help but call them back. When you are a parent, the desire to control and guide can never leave you. Sarika picked up the mat and pillows, walked down tiredly, dropped herself on the bed, and slept.

Kashvi checked if she had packed everything and kept her ticket printout in her bag. She walked out of the room to lock the terrace door when her phone rang. She ran to grab it, but it got disconnected. She quickly scrolled through the numbers in the missed call list and was disheartened to see that number again. She kept looking at the screen and did not dare to call back. She held the phone tightly in her hand and entered the room to sleep. She tightly closed her eyes to sleep, but her mind raced with thoughts, keeping her alert and restless.

She started wiping all unwanted thoughts to sleep peacefully, but it was not easy. Agitated and anxious, she kept glaring at the roof. The past she bore began rolling in front of her, reel by reel.

II
The Meeting

The year was 2008. She had just finished her degree and begun working at a company. Everybody in the family started talking about her marriage. Raghu Uncle (her father's younger brother, who lived in Indore) called and informed her mother about a family they knew and their son. Kashvi was sitting next to her mom and was listening to their exchange of information that was happening at a rapid speed. Raghu Uncle described how handsome the eligible young man is and that he works at a reputable company and earns a generous salary. Mrs. Sharma also found the details interesting and agreed to meet the guy and his family.

As her mother hung up the phone and turned around to discuss things with Kashvi, Kashvi seemed reluctant and passively responded to everything.

Kashvi was annoyed by everything going on around her over the past few months.

Everything had changed after she had started working. As soon as she entered the house, the only conversation her mother wanted to have with her was about marriage proposals. But this time, her mother wanted her to meet the guy, which was even more difficult for her to handle. Having been raised in a conservative family and in a small city, she had not learned to deny certain things. Unwillingly, she agreed to meet the guy.

The next morning, Kashvi was getting ready to go to her office when her mother's phone rang. It was an unknown number, so she handed the phone to her mother and rushed to get the key for her bike. It was getting late for work, so she asked her mom to end the call quickly.

Kashvi scurried down and keyed in to start her bike. She started honking, but it looked like Mrs. Sharma was still on a call. Growing impatient, she urged her to hurry up. "How can you talk so long to an unknown person?"

"It was Praneel's call." Mrs. Sharma said in a delighted tone.

"Who is Praneel?

"He is the same guy who is coming to meet you. Don't you remember? Marriage proposal? Your uncle called yesterday. He is coming tomorrow." Mrs. Sharma informed and notified her at the same time.

"What?" Kashvi exclaimed.

The guy wanted to meet the girl.

On the way to their offices, Mrs. Sharma kept sharing specifics about Praneel and his family. Though most of the details were repetitive, which her mother was passing to her after listening to her uncle, she still kept listening to her mom as a gesture of reconciliation.

"Take leave from the office," Mrs. Sharma gently recommended, and suggested hiding the real reason behind the leave, which was a fiddly task for Kashvi.

Hiding—Was it about respecting privacy or preventing embarrassment in case the proposal is not accepted? She murmured.

She stopped near the bank where her mother worked. "As a parent, I have to take a lead to find a match for you, but it is you who has to think about what you want in your life partner to decide your future with him," Mrs. Sharma added, with a hint of concern while stepping down.

"No decision will be taken without your wish," she said, looking at her daughter's face and certainly, looking curious and eager to hear her reply.

Kashvi was clearly uninterested and pushed her feet to move the bike backward.

"Why do you always leave things half-done? You always forget to close the footrest." Kashvi replied irritably, kicking the footrest back.

She kept thinking about her mother's last two statements, chewing them over all day while working in the office. Every person draws a figure of their life partner, but not many reveal it. Kashvi had seen many ups and downs in her life after her father's demise, which had made her strong. She was honest and had lived her life on her own terms. After her father, she had never left her mother alone. Even if it was a college trip, a party after college, or during office hours, she kept herself away from such trips and outings and used to rush back home. The bleak evenings haunted her, and she always wanted to be with her mother— the fear of losing her mother stayed in her heart after her father passed away. This was the primary reason she never wanted to marry anyone. She knew marriage was a crucial decision, and everyone fantasizes about their life partner.

She, too, had, but the mere thought of leaving her mother alone scared her. After juggling so much around her notions of fear and hope, she decided that, rather than trying to control things, she would go with the flow this time. She applied for leave before leaving the office.

When she reached home, she found her aunt, Shalini, was helping her mom in the kitchen. Her aunt, a distant cousin of her mother, used to visit her home often. Kashvi always found her mother happy in her aunt's company; therefore, she used to feel gratified seeing her at their house. Her visits and talks relieved her mom's sadness. Her aunt was a cheerful lady, and her presence made her mother forget, to a certain extent, all her desolation.

Today again, Kashvi could see the enthusiasm and spark in their talks, but the topical subject between them was only about the guy who is coming to meet Kashvi tomorrow. She wondered what made them so excited about the next day's meeting.

Her aunt was an amalgamation of the old and young generations, whose personality shifted with her surroundings, and she was behind Kashvi in visiting the salon before meeting the guy.

According to her, Kashvi is a pretty girl, but she neglects the beauty regimen that every young girl should follow to impress a guy. Amidst all those chatters, Shalini Aunty kept teasing Kashvi with her silly jokes and singing eighties songs. She kept herself away from her aunt's and mother's powwow and went to the terrace to get some fresh air.

The terrace was her quiet corner, where she found stillness whenever chaos and commotion surrounded her. She would spend hours looking at the roads and the sky.

The road—a long stretch that kept moving no matter how complex or uncertain the path was. The sky—vast and silent, offering space for everyone amid endless tasks.

After spending an hour there, the cool breeze calmed the storm inside her that she had been hiding from everyone since morning.

When she returned and entered her room, she found a stack of dresses kept aside on her bed. Mrs. Sharma and her aunt had raided her cupboard, pulling dresses from each shelf to decide which one would be the right choice for her to wear tomorrow. Perhaps the toughest decision for two women is choosing a dress for the third person.

"I am not wearing any of these dresses. I know what I want to wear. Don't spend too much time on it and focus on what really matters," Kashvi said upfront, signaling her mother.

"See, Jiji, I told you, you are unnecessarily worried about her. She knows everything and waits for the right time for her turn," Shalini said, addressing Mrs. Sharma.

The next biggest question in the house was what to cook for lunch. Mrs. Sharma and Shalini kept discussing the menu, adding and striking items constantly from their list.

Eventually, Kashvi accompanied her aunt to the salon. Kashvi was agitated with all the things going on around her. Still, she kept quiet, as somewhere deep inside, she believed the proposal was destined for rejection. So, let these elders do whatever keeps them happy, especially her mother.

They reached the salon, and the salon lady began engaging with them by asking many questions, which momentarily confused Kashvi.

"Tell me, what type of facial would you prefer? Do you regularly get a facial, or is this your first time? Is it for regular cleanup or for some occasion?"

The last question was disconcerting for her aunt or for anyone who lives in a small city. People can share any secret, but they always keep arranged marriage meetings under wraps, and her aunt pitched in.

"Why do you want to know all this? Definitely, it is for an occasion. Why would someone come so late to your salon?" her aunt replied sarcastically.

Her aunt's snarky reply couldn't stop the salon lady.

"Oh, then it is not for an occasion, but it must be for a special occasion," she smirked and replied in a rhetorical tone.

Kashvi grinned at their argument. She didn't want to be rude, so she interrupted and told the attendant, "There is a function." But people in small cities are never satisfied with short or half information; they want to listen to the whole story and the real reason behind everything. Hence, the salon attendant kept asking, "What kind of function is it? A pooja or some family gathering? Is it at your home or at your relative's place?"

By now, Kashvi, too, was infuriated and asked, "How does it really matter?"

"We can suggest better options," the attendant replied in a tamed voice.

Shalini Aunty jumped in again and replied, "It is for a family gathering, and now, can you please start with your service? It is getting late for us."

It appeared that either her survey form did not contain more questions or she had decoded the customer's requirement, and the attendant had started the service. Shalini kept instructing the attendant about dos and don'ts every few minutes. Somewhere between the arguing and gossiping throughout the service, the attendant and her aunt had become friends by now.

"You can open your eyes now," the attendant asked Kashvi. She opened her eyes and saw some spots twinkling in front of her, as they had been closed for a long time. She heard the attendant saying how pretty she looked, "You are glowing, am I right, aunty?"

Her aunt also answered in the same vein. Kashvi stared at herself in the mirror and did not notice any change on her face. The only noticeable difference she found was the lingering fragrance that had settled inside her nose after a 60-minute massage.

She touched her skin and felt the grains of scrub and cream near her temples, which she wiped off using a tissue placed next to her chair. She then picked up her wallet and settled the bill. Meanwhile, her aunt was still discussing offers and discounts that could be availed on her next visit. Kashvi took her bike from the parking space and called out to her aunt. Once her aunt was seated on the bike, she swiftly rode toward their home.

Within a few minutes, they were at home. She parked her bike and slowly climbed the stairs, whereas her aunt had already reached inside and was talking with her mother, boasting about how the facial had drastically changed Kashvi's face.

Kashvi had a thumping headache; ignoring their trumpets and wows, she hung the key on the keyholder and went to change her dress. Shalini Aunty had already left for her house, assuring Mrs. Sharma that the next day she and her husband would be there after breakfast.

Kashvi sat down with her mother to eat dinner. They didn't talk much at the table. Somewhere, Mrs. Sharma was aware of her daughter's state of mind, and she, too, was puzzled about the next day's meeting.

Being a single parent, she was worried whether she would be able to make all the arrangements in the expected manner. What could her father have done differently to arrange this meeting? Had she made all the required arrangements for tea and lunch? And the most crucial question was—Will she be able to find the right partner for her daughter? With all these thoughts going through her mind, Mrs. Sharma went to sleep.

The alarm rang at six in the morning. Kashvi extended her right arm to turn it off and dozed off again. Subsequently, she heard the pooja bell ringing, pleasant to the ears and awful to open her eyes. Her mother was performing her morning prayer and looked even more devoted than usual. She rubbed her eyes and tried sitting straight.

Her mother's mobile rang, which was kept charging next to her bed. By looking at the last few digits flashing on the screen, she figured out that the call was from the same guy who was coming to meet. Before she could pass the phone, she watched Mrs. Sharma's quick moves, disconnecting her phone from the charging point in the wink of an eye.

It sounded like Praneel had arrived and checked into the hotel.

Her mother had said he would arrive here by 11 AM and then quickly dialed her aunt's phone.

While Mrs. Sharma was on the call with Shalini Aunty, giving her updates about the guy's arrival, Kashvi sauntered to the bathroom. As she entered the bathroom, she heard her mother saying, "Don't forget to wash your hair."

"The outer world must be glowing and glittering, but who cares if the inner world is dark and fake?" Kashvi uttered in a lethargic tone.

When Kashvi was having breakfast, Shalini Aunty arrived and rushed into the kitchen to help Mrs. Sharma, who was busy cooking various dishes. The rich fragrance of lunch had filled the house. The delectable lunch was ready for the guests. Though only the guy was visiting, a delicious spread was prepared for lunch. There were three varieties of curries, dal makhani, poori, and kachori; starters, pulav, chutney, and raita. Ras malai was prepared as a dessert and kept in the refrigerator to serve it cold. A new dining set was taken out, and Shalini Aunty was wiping and arranging the plates and bowls, and double-checking that the right cups were picked up for serving tea.

Mrs. Sharma was making sure everything looked proper in the living room.

Kashvi had dressed up in her cotton kurta and churidar. She tied her long hair in a loose side plait, leaving a few strands and adding a thin elastic band at the end. After so much nudging from her mom and aunt, she wore lipstick. She put on her studs. She looked into the mirror and added a bracelet to cover her bare wrist.

Kashvi was ready but puzzled, and she remained inside her room, reading a book. Her mind was stuck, and somewhere, it was lost, seeing the activities happening around her, which were out of her control.

The doorbell rang, and it was Balraj Uncle (Shalini's husband) who informed Mrs. Sharma and Shalini that Praneel had arrived near their house and that he was going to pick him up. Her aunt rushed into Kashvi's room and informed her to stay inside and not to come out until they called her.

Kashvi felt there was something wrong with her because she did not know what to ask or look for to find the right match in such an arranged meeting, and she was not excited about meeting the guy. She ignored everything and kept reading the book.

The bell rang again, and suddenly there was silence inside the house. The silence was akin to that of a principal or invigilator on rounds during an examination on the school campus — a mix of urgency and a deliberate absence of sound.

Balraj Uncle asked Praneel to take the stairs as the ground floor was empty. He looked at the stairs spiraling and ending toward the verandah of the first floor. The money plants in the exquisite ceramic pots, placed after a few steps, cautioned him to move carefully so as not to damage their leaves. He entered the living room. Mrs. Sharma and Shalini Aunty were anxiously waiting to meet him.

A small window of the kitchen opened into the living room and revealed everything placed on the immaculate kitchen slab. There was a door at the other end of the living room that opened onto a terrace. The door's paint complemented the wall's paint. The vivid-colored cushions on the sofa, the pastel-colored bedsheet with thin white patterns on the Diwan, the bolsters placed perfectly with two small cushions in between, and the small traditional, well-crafted decor on shelves made the room vivacious and beautiful.

After a few minutes of silence, Kashvi heard a hasty yet welcoming conversation, progressing into exclamations and laughter. She heard the clatter of cups and realized tea had been served.

After some time, she heard her aunt calling her name. Kashvi, unaware of the customary approach to arranged meetings, quickly set the book aside, adjusted her dupatta, and walked toward the living room. She entered the room and was not shy. Her fists were closed not in anger, but to calm her reactions. She looked at everyone sitting in the hall, then finally at Praneel.

He was a good-looking and charming young man. He was tall and handsome. He had folded his arms to his chest and was continuously adjusting his watch. On the right side of the couch, he had kept his jacket.

Praneel had noticed Kashvi's fearless entry when she entered the room. Her light-colored dress with an embroidered flaring dupatta was elegant. The studs and small pendant on a sleek, sparkling chain were easy on the eyes. A tiny butterfly hanging at the other end of the bracelet glittered and sometimes sparkled as the rays of light hit its tiny, transparent beads. It brought a smile to Praneel's face.

Her overall personality looked stunning. He kept looking at her, noticing everything while still managing not to make it seem too deliberate.

This was the seventh time; he was meeting a girl on his parents' request. He had always seen girls wearing bright, shimmery Indian attire, such as sarees, with matching bangles and fancy hairdos. This was not the case today.

As Praneel's family was pressuring him to marry, he had met many girls but had turned down their proposals because he had never found someone with whom he could see his future.

He noticed Kashvi found a place near her mom, and she settled herself there.

"I am going out for a while; maybe Praneel and Kashvi can discuss their interests." Balraj Uncle informed Mrs. Sharma and Shalini. Mrs. Sharma and Shalini Aunty sensed the silent cue and moved outside the room.

Praneel was quite prepared for this situation as he had met many girls before meeting Kashvi. However, as it was Kashvi's first meeting with a guy in an arranged meeting setup, she was still wondering why everybody had left the room in haste.

Though Kashvi was naive about arranged marriage meetings, as a cultured and educated girl, she felt that leaving a guest in this way and keeping quiet were probably not cordial ways to welcome any guest at home. Therefore, she ended the silence and filled the void with an impromptu talk, asking Praneel about his journey.

This was the first time they looked at each other directly. Her eyes were shiny and lively, and they spoke volumes about her. He was lost in the sparkling eyes for a few seconds and felt a strong connection with her in those couple of seconds. Her impulsive smile broke the direct eye contact.

"It was good, but finding your house was difficult," Praneel replied.

"It might be, particularly for people who have not lived in a small city. Small cities are unplanned, and you can see markets, residential areas, and illegal constructions all together in one place—no signboards, narrow lanes, and suddenly a wide opening to the main road. But certainly, free from pollution and traffic congestion, unlike big cities," she spoke effortlessly.

"Yes, you are right," he replied cautiously.

In his previous meetings with girls, he was the one who asked questions, and this was the first time a girl had shot the breeze, discussing all sorts of small, random things, which was captivating Praneel.

They kept talking for about 20-30 minutes. Praneel spoke about his education and profession, and she suddenly asked, "Was your placement in this company through the college campus, or did you have to wait and apply through some consultancy?"

This was an untimely and disturbing question for him.

"The girl is evaluating my scores and assessing my acumen without asking direct questions," he spoke in his mind.

"Consultancy," he replied sheepishly, thinking my love at first sight would end with this answer.

"Oh, that is fine. These companies have strategies behind them; they need people who can be trained faster but at the same time at a low cost," she replied.

Praneel was unsure which option he fit into, as neither was impressive.

"Hope you did not mind my mom, uncle, and aunt moving out suddenly. We all could have sat and talked together. Don't you feel so?" she blabbered hesitatingly and knew that she indeed had fallen short of topics now.

He laughed at Kashvi's answer. She looked at Praneel with a fake smile and then turned her face to the door to settle herself again.

Praneel, consciously, kept quiet and waited for Kashvi to speak. He could have asked a lot of things, but he liked the sudden silence in the room and the impulsive response of her to break it deliberately.

"When are you returning to your place?" she asked. "Tonight," he replied in his deep voice.

"How are you going back?" she asked again.

"I have a train tonight. I will reach... sorry, I forgot," he scratched his forehead, trying to recall the name of that city from where he had to board the flight, "in two hours, and then take a flight from there. There are no direct flights from your place today," he replied playfully.

"You don't have enough time for a layover. It looked like this was an unplanned visit," she asked.

"Hmm," what a witty comeback, he thought, and smiled at her response.

"I mean, such unplanned travel needs a lot of planning for office work," she tried correcting her statement.

"Sometimes planning doesn't work, and the best things happen when we are unprepared," he smiled and remarked. In the awkward silences, abrupt questions, and blunt responses, he knew that there was something special between them.

"And it seems like I am here by fate, not by planning," he muttered under his breath and smiled.

After almost an hour, Mrs. Sharma and Shalini Aunty entered the room.

"Hope you had enough time to talk," Shalini Aunty chuckled with a grin.

"Long enough," Kashvi muttered with a tight-lipped smile. Desperate to leave the room, she offered a quick excuse and went into her room.

In a few minutes, Balraj Uncle also joined. He asked Praneel if he was hungry; they could have lunch, otherwise, they could wait for some time. While they were discussing lunch, Praneel got a call from his mother. More than Kashvi's mom and relatives, Praneel's mother was waiting for his response, as he always refused the proposal soon after meeting the girl.

Praneel politely excused himself to talk to his parents. When he came inside, he handed his phone to Mrs. Sharma. Praneel's mother (Mrs. Tripathi) sounded excited and informed Mrs. Sharma that Praneel liked Kashvi. At the same time, she asked Mrs. Sharma to talk to Praneel one more time and confirm whether he had really liked Kashvi. Mrs. Tripathi had heard her son rejecting so many proposals; therefore, she couldn't believe her ears—had she really listened to that right?

Mrs. Sharma paused for a while, holding her phone, and recounted her brief conversation with Praneel—a swift review of whether he is suitable for her daughter —before heading further on this.

"Praneel, I hope that whatever you have conveyed to your mother is a thoughtful decision, and you have not taken it in haste or under any pressure. You can say 'No' if you don't want to get married. Sometimes in such arranged meetings, the guy and girl agree in front of their family, and later regret their decision. You don't have to do the same. It is okay even if you say no; it should be just a thoughtful decision. Meanwhile, I will also talk to my daughter."

And suddenly, Shalini interrupted, "Yes, and even if you say no, we won't send you off hungry."

"This is a careful and final decision, Aunty. Let us check with Kashvi if she is fine with this proposal or not." Praneel replied.

Kashvi was listening from her room and was perplexed, as she had thought Praneel would go back after lunch. She did not expect this guy to be so quick at making decisions. But it was all unexpected for her. What should I tell my mom now? I didn't even give a thought to marrying him. While she was fighting with all kinds of questions, Mrs. Sharma entered the room and informed her about Praneel's decision and asked the same of her.

Behind her question, Kashvi noticed a sense of pride and satisfaction—the rare expressions on her mother's face. The expression that was missing after her father's demise. Kashvi babbled, "Yes, ok!" and Mrs. Sharma didn't wait for further exploration, hurriedly and gleefully, she stepped outside the room.

'It might be that this is how arranged marriages are done.' She spoke to herself.

It was time to share the good news with Tripathis and Sharmas. Both families were happy, especially Praneel's parents, as after rejecting so many proposals, their son had accepted Kashvi. Everybody's phones started ringing, and they were all on calls, congratulating each other and giggling on calls.

Kashvi kept turning the pages of the book, wondering what made him say 'Yes,' and then she questioned herself: "What made me decide so quickly?" She strolled into her room, took out her bracelet, and put on her watch.

"Don't worry, Kashvi, you still have enough time," she spoke to herself.

Shalini Aunty seemed to be the happiest, in fact, happier than Mrs. Sharma, and she was arranging lunch at the dining table. Soon, everybody gathered for lunch, and after the scrumptious meal, cool, delicious rasmalai was served for dessert. Praneel was already full and was reluctant to have more, but Shalini Aunty forced him to have more.

The living room was buzzing with gleeful talk and laughter; conversations moved from one topic to another, a rare moment in the house. She felt a long-forgotten experience had returned to her home.

Praneel asked Mrs. Sharma if he could go out with Kashvi. Suddenly, the gleaming faces turned quiet.

"Do not worry; this won't change my decision. I want to spend some time with her, as I am returning in the evening, and it would be good if I could see this city with her." Praneel watched everybody's reactions and clarified.

Mrs. Sharma looked at Balraj and Shalini, exchanging a questioning glance; they waited, shared glimpses of approval, and agreed. They called Kashvi and asked her to show him some famous places in their city. Kashvi picked up her bike keys when her uncle smiled and gave his car keys to Praneel, and told her to give the bike's key back.

When Praneel was making himself comfortable with the clutch, accelerator, and brake of her uncle's car, he asked Kashvi, "Where should we go first?"

"Temple," Kashvi replied.

"Alright, let us drive toward the temple," he said, smiling. It was not very far from her place and did not take much time to reach. They both went into the temple and sought God's blessing.

Kashvi closed her eyes and prayed, "I am not sure if whatever is happening is right or not. I place my trust in you, God. I believe whatever you have decided and are doing is right for me." She opened her eyes and saw Praneel talking to the temple priest. She quickly bowed before the idol, and they left the temple after taking the prasad.

"What will be our next stop?" Praneel asked.

"There is one more famous temple in this city. Let us go there." Praneel smiled; Kashvi, unaware of the reason, showed him the direction.

It was indeed a divine temple with ancient architecture, and the intricate carvings on its walls and ceiling enhanced its aesthetic appeal. Kashvi told the history behind the temple and its architecture. They roamed in and around the temple and finally stepped out.

While wearing the shoes, Praneel asked, "So, Kashvi, apart from temples, are there any other famous or scenic places to visit in your city?"

"There are many, but those places are pretty far, and it wouldn't be good to go there alone."

"Alone? Can two people be referred to as 'alone'?" he laughed and asked.

Kashvi, mystified at his response, stared at him, but soon she realized his witty remark.

"No, two does not mean alone, but in a small city, it makes a big difference. We can go back home." She answered.

Praneel realized that Kashvi was uneasy, and then he reminded himself to be considerate before voicing his next thought. On the way home, Praneel saw a café with artistic paintings on its walls and asked Kashvi about it. She mentioned that there are very few cafes in this city, and this is one of the famous cafes, particularly known for its Irish coffee and ambience. He immediately slowed down and parked the car.

"At last, there is a place in your city where two people can spend some time alone," said Praneel.

Kashvi understood his indirect expressions, so she got up without saying anything, and they both walked to the café. The interior, lights, and aroma all seemed perfect to him. They ordered their favorite flavors of coffee and looked for a place to sit and talk peacefully.

While they were waiting for their order, Praneel expressed his feelings toward her.

"It was a short meeting, and before leaving, I wanted to be sure whether you liked me." He paused, staring at her.

"Are you happy with this proposal, Kashvi? I know you must be thinking the same. I am not sure if I can articulate it clearly, but I still want to convey what I feel and share what is on my mind now. I have met many girls, and I have never felt the way I did today after talking to you." He laughed slightly, hiding away his shyness.

"Sorry if it sounds awkward, but I am extremely happy after meeting you." He had spoken a lot in his warm voice and now asked Kashvi to tell him whatever she wanted to say right away.

Kashvi could feel her ears getting warmer and her coffee getting colder after listening to Praneel. She kept quiet for a few minutes. She looked up and then replied with a smile, "I am fine with the decision made by my mother." Though Praneel did not get the answer he wanted to hear, he did not want to probe her too much, so he just smiled and stopped his introspection there.

Her eyes were still sparkling, which lit up Praneel's face every time he caught a glimpse of them. They relished their coffee and continued their table talk.

"I don't know how authentic the coffee flavor is; probably you would have had better than this. This is the best coffee that we get in this city," she said.

"It was the best coffee I ever had." He replied and paid the bill.

"It is close to dusk, let us go back home." She said, wiping the glass of her watch.

"Oh, where is that bracelet?" He questioned.

"Bracelet?"

"Yes, the one with a tiny butterfly," Kashvi knew what he was asking, but she was amazed by the details he had noticed about the bracelet.

"The shiny butterfly on your bracelet looked adorable," he added.

She found herself blushing but managed to hide it.

"The butterfly stuck to this dupatta and was ruining its embroidery, so I took it off," and she paced faster toward the car. She found her response inappropriate and quickly opened the car door to sit inside. She made herself comfortable by fastening the seat belt. On the other hand, Praneel keyed in, slowly released the clutch, and accelerated the car toward her house. The car entered a lane that was too narrow, but impish kids were still playing every few meters on the street. A small group of people standing and talking near the houses and shops slowed the drive.

"With all the potholes, narrow lanes, and crowds, who would not have control over the speed, do we really need this many speed breakers?" He asked.

In a few minutes, they reached home. Praneel parked the car in front of her house.

After getting inside the house, Kashvi saw Sarika waiting for them in the living room. She looked, waved at Praneel, and winked at Kashvi.

"She is Kashvi's best friend. She wanted to meet you before you leave, so I called her." Mrs. Sharma introduced Sarika to Praneel. Kashvi went into her room to relax; she was feeling overwhelmed by everyone's response and reactions, especially Praneel's.

"Hope you like our city," Sarika asked Praneel.

"Oh, I must say, it is a pleasant city," he replied in his husky voice.

Kashvi's uncle and aunt went out to bring some sweets for Praneel. They also wanted to give Praneel a gift before he leaves, so they informed Mrs. Sharma that they were going to the market and would return soon. Her mother also went inside the room to pack a Shagun envelope for him—the ritual required in Hindu custom when people enter a new relationship.

Meanwhile, Sarika kept talking to Praneel. She had lots of questions on her mind, and she took this opportunity to assess this guy before her beloved friend got into this relationship.

After 40 minutes, Kashvi came out of her room when the tension melted away, and she realized she shouldn't be hiding herself like this inside the room. She looked at Sarika and signaled her to stop her questionnaire. By that time, her aunt and uncle had returned. They and her mom handed Shagun to Praneel along with other gifts.

"Why are you troubling yourself with these formalities?" Praneel hesitated because accepting those gifts made him feel awkward.

He looked at his watch and informed them that he would take a leave now. Her uncle accompanied him and said he would take him to the station. Balraj Uncle sat in the driver's seat, and Praneel sat next to him.

He looked outside the window to catch a glimpse of her, and they both smiled at each other. This was not a half-hearted smile, but this exchange of smiles radiated a deep warmth on their faces. After the car had moved just a few meters away from her house, Praneel looked outside and waved at Kashvi. In a few minutes, the car was out of everyone's sight. As soon as the vehicle left, Sarika caught hold of Kashvi's shoulders and jolted her.

"He is so handsome, and you both had coffee in that café."

"Who told you this?" Kashvi interrupted her.

"I am good at digging out details," he told me many other things, which you don't know," Sarika replied and winked at her.

"Stop doing that, I know you will start enacting now," said Kashvi. Mrs. Sharma and Shalini Aunty called both of them inside. Sarika was giggling and unceasingly teasing Kashvi.

III

The Departure

Praneel had booked a train ticket for the same night to board an early-morning flight from a city near Gwalior. His plan was to meet the girl and her family, then leave the place to get rid of this setup, as he was tired of meeting girls surrounded by their kith and kin.

Unexpectedly, this meeting was infinitely better. He did not know that he would find his soulmate in Kashvi. He wanted to spend more time with her and felt guilty about booking an early-morning flight.

Balraj Uncle parked the car outside the hotel where Praneel was staying and asked him to bring his luggage. It was already late, so Praneel rushed inside the hotel to complete the checkout formalities. He had only one backpack with him, so he walked briskly to the car, seated inside, and her uncle headed toward the railway station.

Fortunately, they reached the station on time, and Praneel was grateful that small cities have little traffic. He got down, took a deep breath, and could inhale the locomotive smoke. He wanted to inquire about the platform, but Balraj Uncle was more confident about the train's arrival and schedule than the railway staff.

"Do not waste your time here; otherwise, you will miss the train. It is a daily passenger train and won't stop here for long. Follow me, Praneel," he tried to make himself audible to Praneel, who was standing near the inquiry counter, a little far from Uncle. Praneel paced faster and followed him diligently.

"Are you sure about the platform number?" Praneel tried confirming again.

"If not this, then it would arrive at platform number 6. Don't worry, it is next to this platform, not too far," Balraj Uncle panted and replied.

Huffing and puffing, they reached platform number 5. Praneel looked at his watch and noticed it was the train's arrival time. Soon, there was a long, deep sound of a train horn, then chugging and vibration, and, quickly, the platform became busy and noisy with passengers.

Balraj Uncle's eyeballs were moving from side to side with each bogie passing in front of their sight, trying to read the coach number, and suddenly he shouted, "Oh, there it is, come, come, it won't stop here."

At once, Praneel was perplexed, but he quickly adjusted his bag and scooted behind Balraj Uncle. After taking a few yards, they reached the compartment door, where a group of people were trying to get in with their baggage. By the time Praneel could think of something, the uncle extended his right arm to make way, pushing people aside. He caught Praneel's arm with his left hand

and pulled him inside. Praneel felt a wave of force had forcefully pushed him inside. Balraj Uncle had not stopped yet, and he dragged him inside, looked up and down, left and right at the numbers, hopped over a few baggage items lying in the passage, pushed some passengers again to make way, and scolded a few for not giving way.

"45, oh, there it is," he said, and finally they stopped.

Praneel's face had turned red; his hairs were spread in different directions.

"You have to be really quick at the station for these trains. The train stops only for a few minutes, and the crowd won't allow you to get in. Please take your seat, place your bag carefully, and set an alarm, as the train reaches that station at odd hours, I am afraid you might miss the stop. Give a call when you reach your place. Take care and see you soon," Uncle was talking ten to a dozen. Praneel bent to touch his feet, and by the time he looked up, Uncle had reached the gate.

Praneel brushed his hair using his fingers and realized even after so much clamour and chaos, he was not angry. The meeting had changed something in him. His world revolved around his meeting with Kashvi.

Thrilled, happy, and, he wondered what had happened to him. He turned around and made his way back to the seat. It was a window seat, so he kept the bag aside and looked outside the window to see where Balraj Uncle was standing. Uncle was standing a few steps away from the coach, waving at Praneel. The train started, and Uncle gradually disappeared from his sight. As the train sped up, Praneel could only see the dim lights of the faraway houses of the villages passing by the side of the train.

In the excitement, he called his mother.

"Hello, Mom!"

"At last, you remembered me. How many times have I tried reaching you, but you kept disconnecting my call?"

"Oh, don't start again. Hadn't I messaged you?"

"Yeah, you had," she sighed. "I will take some time to adapt. My son's priorities will change now. Am I correct?" Mrs. Tripathi pulled his leg.

"Nothing like that. I will call you after reaching my place."

"Praneel, don't forget to call your father; he is still waiting for your call."

"Ahh, what does he want to know now?" He asked agitatedly.

"Why are you always reluctant to talk to him?" Mrs. Tripathi questioned his son.

"Please don't spoil my peace, Ma." The call ended.

Soon it was pitch-dark. He was tired and noticed all the passengers had fallen asleep. He wanted to sleep, but something was keeping him awake. It was Kashvi's face that appeared in front of his eyes whenever he tried to close his eyes. He tried hard but could not fall asleep.

He took out his mobile and realized he had missed taking her phone number. He thought of calling Mrs. Sharma and asking, but then stopped himself, thinking that would not be appropriate. He slid his phone back inside his pocket, moved down obliquely, and adjusted himself on the berth. He closed his eyes tightly and slowly rewound everything about the meeting.

Every time he tried pondering the questions she had asked, her face flashed, fainting all other things. He rolled to the other side, but the euphoria did not let him sleep. Kashvi's simplicity and intelligence had won his heart.

He kept staring at the people who were in deep sleep and realized he was ecstatic at midnight; a smile was on his face, and the joyful bubbles had not yet settled in his heart.

"Would she be awake? Would she be thinking about me? Would she be feeling the same way I am feeling about her?" After a few questions, he quickly wiped out his thoughts and, being considerate, he brooded, "Let her sleep and take rest." He smiled and closed his eyes to fall asleep.

IV
The Dilemma

At 6 AM sharp, the alarm rang, and Kashvi could hear the pooja bells ringing in her house. There was a small dedicated space for prayer in her room. The prayer space was illuminated with tiny lights and a brass lamp. The brass lamp was filled with oil, and a cotton wick dipped into it, used to continuously light the pristine space. The fresh fragrance of the flowers and incense sticks had mingled and filled the room. The divine place was decorated with hangings made of shiny stones and sequins, the idols of tiny little gods and goddesses, shining in their sparkling ornaments and dresses, were placed adjacent in a row.

With her heavy eyes, she could see her mother carrying the camphor, burning on the brass plate in all the rooms. Placing her palms firmly on the bed, she tried sitting straight on the bed to avoid listening to her mom's morning sermons.

Her mom placed the plate back on the pooja shelf, turned around, her hands still joined, went outside her room, and headed toward the kitchen. Kashvi was surprised to see that her mother had not objected to not getting up at this time. She looked toward the clock to check the time and found it was neither too late nor too early. She yawned and sat quietly for a while on her bed. She pulled her hair, rolled it into a messy bun, and moved clumsily out of her room.

Mrs. Sharma was occupied watching her favorite news channel. The top and bottom of the screen were filled with celestial objects, and different zodiac signs were flashing on the right side of the television screen. With Jupiter, the moon, and Saturn flashing on the screen, the display looked jammed, and the host and astrologer appeared in the center on a compact panel. Kashvi squinted to get a clearer view of the television. The host was full of vim and vigor, shooting questions at the astrologer. The astrologer was predicting the future of different horoscopes as a filler on that talk show. Kashvi rubbed her eyes and settled herself in the next chair.

While Kashvi was wondering why this host had to be so loud on a talk show, she picked up the remote to lower the volume. Mrs. Sharma was carefully listening to his predictions, chopping vegetables, and concomitantly, sipping tea.

"This astrologer is really good, and his predictions are accurate." Mrs. Sharma's tone was steady and sure.

"Last week, for your horoscope, it was shown that you can expect some good news, and I noticed that your marriage is fixed in just one meeting with Praneel."

"Hmm, that is really good news," Kashvi spoke in a derisive tone.

"I also remember he mentioned saying, keep your views to yourself and do not share them with anyone," Kashvi spoke in her subtle tone.

"Yes, so keep it to yourself," her mother replied in a grave voice.

She wanted to remind, 'That was your horoscope, ' but early in the morning, Kashvi felt the heat in her mother's reaction, which had been missing since she woke up.

"Horoscopes, customs, and rituals, everything matters, apart from a person's choice and views. When will these elders look beyond these things? Anyway, the morning seemed a little more normal." She spoke to herself.

The previous day had been extremely busy for them with Praneel's visit. It had taken a toll both physically and mentally and had left Mrs. Sharma exhausted. It was Wednesday morning, and both Kashvi and her mom had to go to their office. Mrs. Sharma was busy with routine chores in the morning, while Kashvi kept moving from the bed to the sofa and from the sofa to the chair until her mother fixed her narrow eyes on her. This was an indication of turning her leisurely morning into a hectic day. With her single stare, she felt recharged in a moment and rushed to get ready for the office.

The awaited day began with the sound of the cooker's whistle, the clang of vessels, the aroma of breakfast, and Mrs. Sharma's constant rants and complaints about how her daughter cleverly avoids kitchen chores. Kashvi was ready for the office and went to the terrace to water some of the plants there.

It was a pleasant and placid day. The cool breeze was blowing gently, and the sun was peeking from behind the clouds, not too strong and not too faint, showering just the right amount of rays on the terrace. She came inside and caught the knob to stop the door from banging loudly because of the cross ventilation in the living room.

When she entered the kitchen to help her mom, she noticed the cooking was almost complete, and her mother asked her to stir the boiling curry while covering the casserole. The breakfast was ready and already dished out on the dining table. In the meantime, Mrs. Sharma's phone rang.

"You use your mobile like a landline phone." Kashvi went blabbering outside the kitchen to bring the phone.

"Can't you keep it with you? I am getting late, Ma." She handed over her phone, showing her discontent.

"Late, really? By the way, who has been passing the time, sleeping on different furniture in the house until now? Bed, chair, sofa; only the center table was left. Mrs. Sharma retorted.

"Wait now, Praneel is calling."

From the other side of the phone, he informed Mrs. Sharma that he had reached Hyderabad on time. Mrs. Sharma seemed enlivened after listening to his voice on the call. Kashvi smiled, looking at her happy face as she talked to Praneel, then went into the kitchen to check on the curry her mother had left unattended, surely in the excitement of talking to Praneel.

Kashvi kept stirring the curry and waited for her mom in the kitchen. When she realized that the expansive dialogue between them was not going to stop, she stepped to the kitchen door and tried to ask in sign language whether the gas stove could be turned off. Her mother was not paying attention to what Kashvi was trying to ask and was more interested in listening to Praneel, so she turned off the gas stove and left the kitchen.

Kashvi waited for her mother at the breakfast table, but it seemed her mother was still on a call with Praneel, and she showed no sign of hunger. In fact, she was not in a hurry to reach the office, despite often complaining to Kashvi about running behind schedule.

Kashvi started nibbling on her breakfast and noticed the newspaper was untouched until now, even though her mother usually read it before going to the office.

"Strange! The morning looks odd without all this. This guy's aura is magical; it has changed everything and everyone in my house in a day. This can be dangerous in the long run." Kashvi grinned and murmured.

She skimmed through the headlines, and eventually, Mrs. Sharma ended the call with a smile and joined her for breakfast.

"He is such a nice and gentle guy. He was asking about everyone, your uncle, aunt, and me." Kashvi was listening carefully but pretending not to care, believing that by evening her mother would get a call from Praneel's parents saying that he liked the girl. But he is not ready for marriage at this point—the usual way of rejecting proposals. She had often heard it happening with her cousins and friends.

"Let me not disappoint my mother in the morning and keep my views undisclosed, as the astrologer has mentioned."

"I am leaving for the office. Call me or message me if you need something." She gulped the remaining tea, which was already cold, and rushed into the room to get her bag.

"If there is something you want to share with me, you can tell me now," her mother questioned, following Kashvi on the stairs.

"This girl is so stubborn," Mrs. Sharma murmured. "Are you happy with this proposal, Kashvi?" she questioned again.

"I am not someone who can make decisions so quickly, but because you and Raghu Uncle have been talking to his family for so long, I believe you would have considered all important aspects before arranging this meeting. I am fine with what you have decided," she answered, dusting her bike, pushing it out, and closing the gate.

In the back of her mind, she was still pondering whether she had made the right decision by telling this to her mother. "Why would a handsome guy like Praneel, working in a reputed firm in a big city, marry a simple girl from a small town?"

She was happy with the proposal and liked Praneel, but was somehow scared of disappointment; therefore, she kept herself away from the trending topic about her marriage. She had not been paying attention to the talks surrounding her and Praneel since yesterday.

In the office parking area, she found Sarika waiting for her.

"Feels like I woke up on a different planet today," she muttered while she loosened the straps and carefully pulled her helmet off.

"What do you mean? I am always on time; it is you who always arrives before time," Sarika replied confidently. They both locked their bikes and helmets and walked into the office.

ppp

On the other side of the country, in Hyderabad, Praneel had reached his office and was catching up on emails after his leave. He kept scrolling through emails, switching between tabs, and after realizing he was unable to focus, he decided to take a tea break. He called his friend Akash. They both proceeded to the cafeteria to have tea. The cafeteria was busy and crowded. It was peak hour for employees to have the hearty meal of the day, and on Wednesday, the busiest day, the cafeteria seemed chock-a-block with employees. They both looked for a place to sit and talk placidly, making the most of their few minutes of break.

"So, what's up?" asked Akash.

Praneel smiled. He placed the cup on the table and looked outside.

"How was the meeting?" Akash asked again. Akash was Praneel's close friend, and Praneel had informed him about his visit to meet Kashvi.

"It was good." He paused. "I liked the girl, and I have informed my parents of the same," said Praneel.

"Wow! Nice one, finally it is time to celebrate," said Akash.

Praneel looked up, the elated expression clearly prominent on his face.

"I don't know, it is a strange feeling, Akash. From the time I met her, I couldn't keep my mind off her. Since last night, I have only been thinking about her. I was so exhausted that I wanted to take leave today, but I am so restless that I cannot sleep. Every time I close my eyes, I see her face. I really don't know what has happened to me. I have come to the office, but now I am unable to focus on my work, too," he explained with gusto and exhaled.

Akash started laughing with a gulp of tea in his mouth, and he managed not to spit it out.

"Am I sounding funny or dramatic?" Praneel asked.

"No, I was recalling what you told me before going to meet her. You had made this sudden visit just to oblige your parents' request because you were tired of meeting these girls. But look at you now. You got caught in the trap," he smiled. "There must be something special in her," added Akash.

"Yes, you are right, but I won't call it a trap. I am glad that I met her. The best thing that had ever happened to me." He paused for a while.

"Let us talk about something else. I don't want to talk about her now, I mean I want to, but," he muffled, refrained from talking further, and smiled.

"You will be fine. Call and talk to her," suggested Akash.

"I forgot to take her phone number," he replied with regret in his voice.

Akash feinted a punch toward Praneel, "then sit and wait until you get her number."

"Will she be feeling the same about me?" He asked curiously.

"Maybe or may not be. You need to talk to her," answered Akash.

While Akash left to go back to work, Praneel decided to call at home.

"Ma, it's me." (He had called on the landline, and he heard someone clearing their throat.) It was his father.

"Where is mom?" He inquired.

"Praneel, don't be so strong-headed that you forget to respect your elders." Mr. Tripathi spoke.

"Why do you always feel that I am disrespecting you. I am just asking about Ma.

"Forget it, tell me the reason for calling at this time." Mr. Tripathi stopped him in the middle of the argument and made an attempt to understand why he had called.

"Nothing, I wanted to talk to her. I will call later."

"Anything else?" Mr. Tripathi probed again. He took some time to respond.

"I liked Kashvi, Pa! You can get the marriage date fixed. Praneel completed his sentence with some hesitation.

"Good to know. I had lost all hope after seeing the conflicts between you and your mother's choices." Mr. Tripathi remarked.

"I have to get back to my work," and the call got disconnected.

Praneel plugged in his headphones and played music to distract himself. He realized the lyrics of the songs were giving words to his feelings.

"There was some magic in her eyes," he stroked his hair and murmured. He smiled at himself again and continued working.

Meanwhile, in a city in Madhya Pradesh, Sarika was eager to hear something about Praneel from Kashvi.

"Now tell me, has he called you after reaching his place? What did he say?" Sarika irked her with her questions.

"Who?" asked Kashvi.

"Don't you know who I am referring to? Don't be so boring," Sarika replied.

"No, I am clueless. What are you asking, and why are you asking? Please tell me," she stopped walking. Sarika held her hand and pulled her to the side.

"I am asking about Praneel," she said under her breath.

"Oh, you guys need to slow down and put a pause on this.

"Anything happened?" Sarika asked with concern.

"You never know these guys. Everyone who comes and meets you at your place will be amicable. Why and how will someone deny you to your face, even if they don't want to marry? You are also behaving like my mother." Kashvi spoke at length without a break.

"Hey, hold on. Everything happened in your presence, and you know nobody forced him. It was he who spoke to his parents first, and then they conveyed the same to your family."

"He had a whole day to express his views; moreover, I could see the affection and honesty in his eyes, which is indubitable," said Sarika and paused.

"When would you stop doing this, Sarika?"

"Stop doing what?"

"Looking into the eyes of guys," Kashvi pulled her friend's leg.

"This was for a different reason," Sarika replied playfully.

They both looked at each other, and the argument faded into their laughter. Sarika's desk was right behind Kashvi's, so she spent the whole day pestering Kashvi with her pretentious jokes and twaddle about Praneel.

They were childhood friends and were inseparable. Both sprightly and humorous, but still poles apart when it comes to expressing their feelings — Sarika, an outspoken personality. In contrast, Kashvi was reticent and hardly shared her feelings with anyone except her dear friend Sarika. They were each other's confidante.

It was 6 PM, and people in the office had begun slowly leaving for the day. After finishing their work, they both locked their systems and left the office.

When Kashvi entered her house, she threw her bag on the sofa and went into her room. She opened her closet and scanned the dresses to pick the one that didn't need ironing. She pulled out a dress from the first shelf and nudged the door using her elbow. She ensured that her mother had not watched her doing this. Her mother was on a call, sitting in the corner of her bed in the same room, happily talking to someone.

"Looks like it was a busy day for her over the phone," she whispered.

Sharing some announcements and choices, and making some declarations, Mrs Sharma had caught her daughter's words but avoided responding.

By the time she had freshened herself up, her mother was in the kitchen, and the aroma of tea had filled the living room. Mrs. Sharma was pounding ginger, black pepper, cloves, and cardamom, which she usually adds after the first boil of the tea. She heard her mother humming a song after a long time.

"Oh ho, the magic is still there."

"Mrs. Tripathi had called today." Mrs. Sharma turned around and informed Kashvi.

"Your 'to be mother-in-law." Mrs. Sharma made a playful remark.

"Praneel seems very happy after meeting you; Mr. and Mrs. Tripathi will meet us in Indore for a small function, but they want the wedding to be held only in winter."

The tea tasted perfect with all the good news her mother had just shared with Kashvi.

"What is this next meeting for?" Kashvi asked.

"His parents want to meet you, as I met him, and every parent has the right to do so," her mother reacted.

"Yes, then why didn't they all come together?" Kashvi asked a valid question that her mother easily ignored.

"You always have inimical reactions to everything. The meeting is not for meeting; it is for conducting the pre-wedding ritual — 'roka.'" Mrs. Sharma responded.

"The meeting is not for meeting — you guys are really confused," Kashvi mocked. She dipped the biscuit in the tea; it broke and melted in the cup before she could eat it.

"Never buy this biscuit again; it spoiled my tea."

"You know the store; nobody had stopped you from buying the one that you like." Her mother could read between the lines and retorted.

With a look of disapproval, Kashvi carried the cup to the kitchen and placed it in the basin for washing.

She put the saucepan on the burner to prepare another cup of tea.

"Do you want another cup of tea?"

"If there is extra, I can have," her mom replied—a very standard response of every tea-lover in India.

She brought one cup to her lips to taste and grabbed the other cup by its brim for her mother. The tea was piping hot and had burned her tongue, and the brim was too hot to hold the other cup.

"You can use a tray instead of struggling so much; this requires common sense." Stating so, Mrs. Sharma took the cup away from her hand.

Kashvi knew this was an indirect satire of her questioning about the meeting.

Mrs. Sharma's phone started ringing again. It was Praneel's call.

"Namaste, Aunty!"

"Bless you, beta! You have called at the right time. I was telling Kashvi that Mrs. Tripathi had called; she was checking on the marriage date."

Wow! He exclaimed, and then controlled his reaction.

Following the discussion, Praneel had gathered the courage to ask for Kashvi's phone number.

"Oh, she is sitting right next to me," replied Mrs. Sharma, handing her the phone. Kashvi was not prepared and held the phone with a tepid look.

"Hello."

"Hi Kashvi, I forgot to take your phone number yesterday. Hope you don't mind sharing it now," he inquired.

"Umm, no, I mean, yes. I will text you."

"Would you mind sharing it now? I will note it down." He did not want to delay it any further.

"Oh, ok then, note it down, it is ...," said Kashvi.

"Noted, thanks. It is time to leave the office now. I will

call you after reaching home. Catch you later," Praneel said in haste yet in a delighted voice.

"Yes, bye," Kashvi replied. The call dropped.

"Next time, please ask before handing such calls to me."

"Sure, I will see if I get a call hereafter," she stressed on the last word and smiled. Mrs. Sharma took her phone back and passed Kashvi's mobile to her.

"See, you've just received a message. It might be from Praneel."

Kashvi checked her message and noticed her mother's assumption was correct. She turned pink and straightened her lips to conceal her smile.

She read the message from Praneel.

'Is that you?'

She messaged: 'Yes'.

He texted back, adding a smiley.

Kashvi made herself comfortable on a chair, set the phone aside, and unfolded the pages of the book. At short intervals, Mrs. Sharma's phone kept ringing. Her daughter's news of her marriage had already spread through the family, and the curious Sharmas were keen to know every minute detail about Praneel and his family. Some of them were overjoyed with the news, a few were envious of seeing everything fall into place so easily, and a handful of them were green-eyed and anxious to see how Mrs. Sharma would make arrangements for marriage.

In silence, Kashvi watched the conversations. "People participate in your happiness for different reasons; not all of them celebrate your achievements and milestones." She smiled and got lost in her book.

At the dinner table, Mrs. Sharma's inner conflict found expression in her words. "It is his blessing that everything is happening so easily and smoothly. Searching for a groom is not an easy task, and on top of that, for a single parent, it is even tougher. I had not thought that your marriage would be fixed so easily. People have so many demands and expectations, especially when they are looking for a bride for their only son. Your father had planned so many things for you, but life takes unexpected turns. Things would have been different if your father had been there."

Mrs. Sharma always thought of her husband and remembered him at least once a day. Kashvi just listened to her inner thought, knowing this was the only way to comfort her mother.

Occasionally, Mrs. Sharma would also push away half-eaten plates and go back to sleep, holding memories of her husband, but she had eaten her dinner this time.

Kashvi was very close to her father; she lost him in an accident. More than 12 years have passed, but she still feels that she lost him just a few months ago.

"The mind preserves memories like precious jewels; you open that vault and revisit it, and you see that they remain unfaded and untouched." She recalled her days with her father.

To take her mind off it, she opened her cupboard and started sorting dresses from a stack; her phone rang. Kashvi was startled by the sudden sound; moreover, nobody called her late at night. She glanced at the screen and saw it was Praneel's call. Kashvi picked up the call.

"Hello!"

"Hi, Kashvi!"

"Hi!"

"Some of my friends had come, and by the time they left, it was late; otherwise, I would have called you a little early."

"That's fine. Anyway, I was not expecting your call." She blurted out.

Oh! He responded in a slight shock.

"I mean, it was too late," she attempted to correct her statement.

If you are tired, we can talk tomorrow, he spoke in a subdued voice.

"Yes, I want to sleep. Bye!"

Her candid response startled Praneel.

She heard "bye" in a faint voice from the other end of the phone and disconnected the call.

Praneel had not anticipated this response and had experienced the quickest call of his lifetime. Even disconnecting a call from a salesperson in the banking sector takes a little longer than this call.

He looked at the clock hanging in his room to check if it was really too late to call someone. He smiled after looking at the time; it was 9:23 PM. He turned on his laptop to watch a movie. He picked up his mobile, lying next to his laptop, and texted "Good night" to Kashvi.

Praneel waited for a few minutes and then realized she had really fallen asleep.

The whole day had been hectic for him, too, and he had forced himself to stay awake to talk to Kashvi. Now, as she had slept, he crashed out in bed.

ᘏᘏᘏ

Week 2

A few days passed, and Praneel began calling her in the evenings or at night after office hours. These calls always ended in less than five minutes. The conversations lacked the warmth and connection that Praneel wanted to feel, which gradually mounted stress in his heart.

The more he tried to engage her in discussion, the greater the distance he felt when assessing her responses.

One night, Kashvi got another call from Praneel. This time, she was aware that she could not give the usual excuses to end the call quickly, and she had to be on the call for at least a few minutes longer than usual. When she answered the call, Praneel took a dig.

"Are you sleepy today, too?"

"That's alright, we can talk. I can manage and can sleep a little late today." Kashvi answered, oblivious to his question.

"How late?" he asked wittily.

"10-15 minutes should be fine," she replied.

Praneel wanted to laugh, but he discerned the innocence in her reply and changed the topic.

Praneel thought Kashvi might be as curious as he was about her and would ask, but when he experienced the hush moment and heard nothing from the other side of the phone, he consoled himself that maybe her sleep clock was ticking on her end.

He continued to keep the conversation going, but soon noticed the long pauses and flat answers from the other side unless he prompted.

"Hope you are still awake?" he asked.

"Oh yes, I am."

Praneel started discussing his mundane routine, his office hours, and asked the same about her. He was purposely yet discreetly continuing the conversation because he was aware of her demure nature and wanted to know more about her, and, more importantly, to understand what would be the right time to call her. In the last few weeks, they had hardly talked for an hour collectively, which was troubling Praneel.

She answered everything about her office, her role in the office, and how she handles other things at home with her mom. She sounded tired, and with her short and vague responses, Praneel knew she was uninterested in talking and wanted to sleep now.

"You sound tired and sleepy. Talk to you tomorrow," he said.

"Yes, sure"

The call disconnected, leaving Praneel with a question.

"Is she doing it intentionally?"

V
The Acceptance

The following week, when Kashvi reached the office and took her phone out of her bag, she saw a few missed calls from Praneel.

After seeing those calls, she started thinking, what could be the reason for calling at this time? Is there something urgent? When she was absorbed in her thoughts, someone patted her shoulder. It was Sarika, smiling mischievously at her.

"Finally, I caught you fantasizing about Praneel," she cleared her throat.

"The unspoken words, the ruthless office environment, and these phone calls—oh, these countless obstacles between us." Sarika tried to end the last few lines as a couplet and snatched her mobile.

"Shut up!" Kashvi spoke, sticking a note on her desk.

"Oh, my goodness, so many missed calls and no replies," she added.

"Check your inbox first; there are so many unread emails. You really don't have any work." Kashvi replied, taking her phone back from her friend's hand and keeping it aside.

"Who woke you up today?" Kashvi was bemused and looked at Sarika's face.

"Who was supposed to do that? Had you hired someone to do that for me?" Kashvi replied.

The lady sitting next to them stared icily at them for the disturbance.

"Sorry," Kashvi apologized to her and nudged Sarika with her elbow.

"Let us go for tea." Kashvi and Sarika left their desks and headed toward the cafeteria.

ppp

Praneel and Akash were in a meeting with the other team members. During the meeting, Akash's phone was buzzing, which he silenced with a message.

"Why don't you answer her call?" Praneel spoke to his friend in a hushed, slightly agitated tone.

Akash ignored and observed that the stress lingered on his friend's face.

When the team went out for a tea break, Praneel didn't talk much at the table.

"What happened? Are you alright?" Akash asked when everybody left the table.

"Yes," answered Praneel.

Akash got a call again. It was his girlfriend's call.

"Let me take this call. I will join in a few minutes." He replied. Praneel nodded in response.

Praneel looked at his phone, and there was no call or message from Kashvi until now.

His mind overflowed with questions, making him anxious. "Is she really interested in me? Is she really tired to take calls at night? Or is she deliberately doing this to avoid talking to me? What if she had lied in front of her mother and everyone?"

"It had been more than ten days now, and she had not called me even once." Praneel looked mystified.

Akash ended the call with his girlfriend and returned to the table.

"Yes, tell me now. What happened?"

"Nothing, work stress," Praneel avoided his question.

"This doesn't look like work stress. Have you fought with Kashvi?" Akash asked.

"Who fights over a call? Anyway, it had only been a few weeks. Moreover, she should first talk to fight with me," replied Praneel.

"What do you mean by this?"

"I mean, she doesn't talk much, so I was thinking if she likes me or not," he sounded flustered.

"If you feel so, better talk to her today," Akash suggested.

"I think I am scared. What if she says she doesn't like me?" Praneel ran his hand through his hair in stress.

"You are overthinking, Praneel, and this is something that is out of your control."

"I felt drawn to her."

"Call her and sort it out. Come, let us go back." Akash patted his shoulder.

"You go ahead. I will sit for a few more minutes," Praneel answered.

After Akash left, Praneel called Mrs. Sharma. She picked up the call after a few rings.

"Hello, Aunty! "Are you busy?"

"I am in the office, but we can talk."

Praneel paused for a few seconds, but then, without wasting much time, he asked her if she had sought Kashvi's opinion about him.

"Is she happy with this proposal? It should not be just a one-sided decision," he added.

"Oh, yes. I had definitely taken her views. Actually, the same night, when you left for your place, I discussed it with her again. And she agreed to it. May I know the reason behind this concern?" She asked Praneel. He paused.

"I don't know, but this thought has been haunting me for the last few days. I have seen this happen with girls, where parents don't bother about a girl's choice and give preference to the guy's choice, so I thought I would call and talk to you. I hope I have not bothered you."

"Oh, not at all, good you called me. It is always good to call and talk upfront rather than keeping things inside and making it worse."

Before Praneel could hang up the call, Mrs. Sharma added, "I understand why you got this thought. I don't know whether it's right to say Kashvi is reserved, but she is definitely not good at expressing herself. I will speak to her; you don't need to worry about it."

"No need to talk to her. I will only talk to her. I was only concerned if you had taken her views into account or not, and please don't hesitate even once if you or she feels that I am not the right guy for her."

"Wipe those thoughts from your mind and focus on your work, Praneel. There is nothing like that. In fact, I am happy that you called and talked to me directly about this. I have found the right partner for my daughter."

A slight smile tugged on his lips, hearing her last sentence. As he spoke to Mrs. Sharma, he felt a sense of relief. The burden he had been carrying for the last few days had lifted. However, he still had some qualms lingering in a corner of his mind, which could only be dispelled by talking to Kashvi. He decided to speak with Kashvi that same night.

Returning to his workstation, he put on his headphones and started working. Although he wanted to talk to Kashvi, he resisted the urge. He refrained from calling or messaging Kashvi that day after speaking with her mother.

On the other hand, Mrs. Sharma called Sarika to inform her about Praneel's call. She wanted Sarika to talk to Kashvi as they were close friends, and Kashvi only talked openly with Sarika. As they grew up, she had seen them share emotions and support each other at different stages of their lives.

Everyone has only one friend with whom they can talk their heart out without being judged. Sarika assured Mrs. Sharma, saying she would talk to Kashvi and sort things out. She need not worry about this subject anymore.

After lunch, Sarika and Kashvi were strolling inside the office campus when Sarika asked Kashvi if she had called Praneel back. Kashvi shook her head in response, which made Sarika angry because she had seen his missed calls on Kashvi's phone in the morning.

"Do you really want to marry him, or is someone in your family forcing you to go through with this marriage?" Sarika asked anxiously.

"Why are you asking this?" asked Kashvi.

"That guy calls you two or three times a day, and you don't even call him back once. If you are in the office and you don't feel like talking from here, at least message him. You need to understand his feelings too. I know it has only been a few weeks, but that is how relationships grow and become stronger. It cannot be that one person is concerned, trying to approach and making an effort to understand, but the other is not putting in any effort," said Sarika.

"Why do you feel so? Because I did not call him back, you empathize with him, and how do you know all this? Have you called him?" Kashvi suspected.

"Of course not, why would I do that?" she replied.

"You can do that, I know you," she grinned.

"And I know you. I can see this, and I don't have to call someone for it. You are not so tied up with work that you cannot spare a few minutes to talk to him. It is always a give-and-take. What if he doesn't call you?" Sarika asked.

"I will be relaxed," Kashvi replied in a bleak voice.

"It is easy to say this now, maybe because you are not close to him yet. I will ask the same question when you are deeply in love with him. I bet you will regret the response that you just blurted out in front of me." Sarika paused.

"He likes you, and he has called your mother. He feels that you are marrying him under some family pressure. Please tell me if you really feel so. I will inform your mother."

Kashvi was quiet and waited for a small group of people to pass by, who were also strolling during the lunch hour.

"No, it is nothing like that," she replied.

"He is a nice guy. It is just that maybe I have never given a thought to it, and all these things are happening at a fast pace. To tell you the truth, I am afraid, Sarika."

"Afraid of what?"

"I am apprehensive about this proposal. What if, for some reason, all this doesn't work as planned and gets canceled?"

"Why would this happen? Why do you always consider the negative side first? Can't you be positive? You definitely have something on your mind. Tell me now," questioned Sarika.

"I am cognizant of the mindsets and choices of people living in society. People are educated and live in a modern society, yet their mindset and attitude have not changed. Though they say they want their son to get married to an educated and cultured girl, they are always concerned about their appearance."

"Like what?" Sarika probed her.

Kashvi took a deep breath and continued.

"I have seen people's inclination toward superficialities rather than giving preference to other significant traits of an individual; the physical appearance takes precedence over a person's attitude, character, and knowledge. I know it is an individual's choice, but." She went quiet. "Praneel won't be thinking on the same line, but what if his parents have a concern?"

"Wait, wait! What is the problem? I still don't understand what you are trying to say. What concern are you referring to?" Sarika looked bumfuzzled as she listened to her friend's perspective.

"I am talking about my dusky complexion," she clarified in a dull tone and halted under a shady tree. The leaves rustled as the gentle breeze blew, and she fixed her hair, tucking it behind her ears.

"What? Has anybody told you anything? Why do such unpleasant thoughts dwell in your mind? You look beautiful," Sarika spoke, pacing her speed to reach where Kashvi was standing, keeping her voice noticeable and yet not loud.

"I am sharing what I have seen happening in our society," Kashvi meddled with her views and stopped her friend from giving any further justification.

"People reject some girls because of their height, color, and whatnot," Kashvi replied sternly.

"Don't you remember what happened to our college friend? That young man's family had such a lame excuse that her nose was not sharp. That, too, they realized after their engagement," she said snarkily.

"I still remember how devastated she was. Having been acquainted with all such instances, I definitely don't want to get into such circumstances, live in a false world, and regret it later. I have decided that until I meet his parents, I don't want to get involved with him and carry a burden of guilt for life-long," she added, walking on the side pathway.

"Not everyone is the same, Kashvi. Don't overthink and ruin things. He likes you, and I saw that when I met him. I talked to him for almost an hour because I knew you both wouldn't have much time to talk in front of your uncle and aunt."

Sarika paused for a while.

"Remember, Aunty had called me so that I could meet him as well. She is so considerate; hardly anyone's parents do that. They meet and secretly fix marriages, revealing only to the third person after engagements. Just think, why would she have called me? She knew I could talk and observe what you would not be able to do in front of your relatives and sometimes in the presence of parents, too. She wanted to take the opinion of someone close to you, who is also in the same age group and has the same thought process."

"When I asked him what he liked the most about you, he mentioned that he had met many girls. They were all pretty, but most of them were meek. Though they were all well-educated, they hardly asked anything that made sense, and their unctuous attitude did not go well with him. On the other hand, when he met you, you started the conversation without a qualm. It made him feel like he was in a congenial place, and surprisingly, your questions were not about marriage plans, his work, or his salary. Listening to your casual, unguarded responses, he felt he was talking to someone he knew, which made him comfortable about his visit and the meeting. Gradually, your questions about his career and other details amused him. He was charmed by your calm and sensible approach." Sarika explained what she and Praneel had discussed that evening.

Kashvi was staring at the bricks lined up on the office lawn and listening carefully to her persuasive speech.

"We have exceeded our break hours. It is getting late. Let us get back to work now," she said and smiled at Sarika.

Before Kashvi could step forward, Sarika called her from behind.

"Kashvi, he also mentioned one more thing about you."

Kashvi raised her eyebrows in question.

"He said he felt an immediate connection between you and him when he looked at you for the first time. Though he had told everyone at noon that he liked the girl, he decided in the café while talking to you that you are the one he wanted to marry and spend his life with."

Kashvi smiled, and her cheeks turned red. "You have a knack for extracting information from others. You should have been an informant or a reporter." Kashvi said, turning to Sarika. They both walked briskly into the office building and returned to their desks to work.

After dinner, Kashvi went for a walk with her mother. She knew that after Sarika, it was now her mother's turn to advocate why she should not avoid answering Praneel's call.

"He is calling to be in contact with you, and this is the way to understand each other before marriage. I believe we mutually agreed on this relationship. Haven't I asked you? Are you still on the fence and not ready to get married?" Kashvi kept walking, looking at the ground, and staying quiet when her mother questioned her. She knew everything her mother was trying to explain, but she didn't speak about the concerns she had shared with Sarika.

"No matter how much you try to hide, I am your mother, and a mother understands her child's feelings by observing their gestures; I know you like him. Kashvi agreed with what her mother just said, but frowned at her when she referred to her as a 'child'."

"Don't give me that look, you are still my child," her mother repeated.

If you are busy, you can discuss when the right time is to connect, or at least drop a message. This is also basic phone etiquette; you are not too young to be explained again. It is not some random call from your friend that you can avoid or answer based on your mood. Small mistakes can create big misunderstandings in a relationship. For now, it is Praneel; you need to be even more careful when dealing with his parents and other family members. When you decide to marry someone, it is obvious that the two people will talk and spend time together. In your case, you are not in the same city to meet frequently to know and understand each other; therefore, calls are the only way to be connected." Her mother explained to her, and after half an hour, they returned home.

She felt that she was carrying a significant burden on her shoulders now—the task of talking to Praneel. When she returned to her room and glanced at her phone screen, she noticed two missed calls from Praneel. As she was looking at the screen, the phone rang again.

The conversation began with a polite greeting.

As he spoke about his day-to-day work, she remained attentive this time, keeping an eye on the clock to make the conversation last longer than their previous calls. She wanted to hang up, but with all the preaching she had received from her mother and her friend, she refrained and responded in a dull tone.

In these few weeks of palaver, where Kashvi was disinterested and had hardly noticed anything about Praneel, on the contrary, he had paid heed to every word Kashvi spoke, what she emphasized, her cautious or keen participation, and her impassive tone. He can easily make out how she feels listening to her responses.

"What happened, Kashvi? Is there anything bothering you? You sounded upset."

She was astonished at how he figured it out. She was startled for a minute and then looked at her phone.

"Yes, I am upset," she replied without mincing her words.

"May I know the reason?" he asked. Kashvi wanted to say, "You are the reason," but then she measured her statement and took a deep breath.

She could no longer control her words at this time.

"You call me three to four times a day, you could have asked me, why do you need to complain to my mother?" she replied, losing her patience.

"Wait," he interrupted her. "I did not complain. I just asked her. And out of four times, you only pick up my call at night, and there too, you are half-asleep most of the time, so what do you expect now? Anybody in my place would have this question. Isn't it obvious?"

There was a pause as usual.

"Now, see, what is the meaning of this silence? How can a person on the other end of the call figure out? I am sure you will fall asleep in a few minutes. You better go and sleep. We will talk tomorrow. You love your sleep more than anyone else. Good night!" The call ended abruptly.

Praneel's lengthy lecture had jolted her, and she was awake now. She realized he was right; she loves to sleep, at the same time, she also experienced how it feels when someone disconnects the call when you are willing to talk.

"It is so disrespectful." She muttered.

She looked at her mobile; the call had ended in 12 minutes.

"Not bad." She smiled proudly at herself, exceeding the standard call limit. She was unsure whether to call him back or go to sleep.

"It is a bad day for me. Why is everyone overreacting? And why am I being reprimanded for not calling and talking to someone late at night?"

'A guy calling a girl frequently is considered an anomalous behavior in Indian society. Besides this, their parents strongly object to responding to these calls, especially when they are from their girlfriend or boyfriend. On the contrary, when their parents arrange these meetings and marriages for their son and daughter, the situation is different. The parents put in all their efforts to bring them together. The concept of arranged marriage is peculiar.' She folded her arms around her knees, waited for some time to pass, and then buried her face in the pillow to sleep.

Praneel kept his phone aside. He was a short-tempered guy and was aware of how his anger could affect his relationship with her. As the time passed, he decided to clear this dilemma without wasting much time, and he rang her up again.

"Don't worry, I won't take much time. I have a question, answer that and sleep," Praneel stressed on the last word of his sentence.

"Do you like me or not?" Praneel asked. The line went quiet.

"I am reaching out to get to know you more, but if you don't like me and you don't want to marry me for any reason, you can confess right away. I can inform my parents and your mother as well. I know that you are mature enough to understand that this will not only spoil your life but mine too."

"See, you didn't even interrupt me in this whole conversation." He sighed in anticipation of her reply.

Kashvi felt she was really guided by some evil star today. "The less I want to talk, the more people are probing me to talk." She spoke to herself.

"I cannot wait long. Just speak what is on your mind. I had asked the same thing in the café." He reminded.

As far as I understand you, you are not indecisive, and you will never hesitate to say no and hold back something. None of us should be, especially when the question is about spending your whole life with someone. Do you need more time, Kashvi?

"No," she replied.

"What do you mean by 'no'?" He asked impatiently this time, keeping his fingers crossed.

Sarika's words echoed in her mind, and she thought maybe her overthinking would really spoil things. She thought quickly and did not want to go deep into these arguments, and said, "I mean, nothing like that. I want to marry you."

"It is just," she paused and reformed her statement.

"It happened in haste, and I really don't know what to say. Perhaps I didn't expect that. Why on earth would you want to marry me, and how can it happen in such a short meeting?"

"I find it difficult, and it is not easy to talk." She sounded low this time.

She wanted to share her concern that she had spoken in front of Sarika, but stopped herself and ended her statement.

Praneel's heart had almost sunk when he heard 'No' from Kashvi at the first instance. He realized he had been a little hard on Kashvi, which was not correct.

Praneel knew he had to start over again. It had been only a few weeks, and he could not expect Kashvi to open her heart.

I didn't want to argue; I just wanted to know if you're happy with this proposal.

"Yes, I understand." Her voice trembled.

His anger was replaced with guilt.

"I think it is too late for you, and we can talk tomorrow," suggested Praneel.

"Yes," and she hung up the call without waiting.

This tiff had left her dull. She had sensed the anger in his voice when he had questioned her response. She knew she was not good at pleasing people by talking, whether to friends or relatives, and she had spoiled things with her stern, straight responses. However, she was happy with whatever Praneel had spoken so far. The two most important things she had figured out in the call today.

First: how he figured out she was upset merely by talking for a few minutes on the call. Second: being honest about his concern and discussing a matter to the point.

"If I really do not care about him, why am I feeling low? Have I started liking him? Is this the beginning of me falling for him?" She questioned herself.

On the other hand, Praneel was cheerful and full of energy. With a winsome smile on his face, he kept recalling her words, "I want to marry you."

His heartbeat was faster this time, but he was unhappy with the way he had talked to Kashvi today and wanted to apologize. He picked up the phone and texted her. The phone buzzed, and Kashvi picked it up to read the message. She knew it must be Praneel's good night message.

Thank you for accepting me and for being who you are! Good night.

Kashvi read the message and smiled. She typed, Good night!" and this time, she added a smiley, too.

VI
The Budding Relationship

The spring was peaking in slowly, and the temperature had started rising daily. The sun was up and shining brightly, and the lawn was covered with lush green grass and appeared slightly damp. The potted plants, placed every few yards on the sidewalks, were blooming with vibrant flowers, and the flowerbeds on both sides of the lawn had become dense and colorful. The bougainvillea hanging on the boundary wall had spread its branches, and with the rising temperature, its bright pink flowers had begun to bloom. The sand in the unused space glistened with the rays falling upon it. The terrace door was still closed; the sun rays were sneaking inside the living hall through the gap in the door. The floral fragrance spread throughout the house, rejuvenating the senses.

A paperboy had thrown the newspaper. It banged on the door and landed on the balcony. The sound woke Kashvi, and she felt refreshed. A smile flashed on her face, and she looked stunning. She went onto the balcony to pick up the newspaper. It was tied with a thread and was lying in a corner. She untied it, tried to uncurl it as she entered the living room, then placed it on the center table. Keeping the weight on both sides of the newspaper, she recalled Praneel's message from last night and smiled to herself with quiet affection.

"What is for breakfast?" she asked, slouching against the kitchen door and waiting to see what her mother was preparing for breakfast. Mrs. Sharma was lining up the plates in the crockery section and answered, "I have not decided yet."

She stretched languorously.

"Oh, I know what I will get to chew today," she blabbered, then headed toward the bathroom to take a shower.

Her mother was rolling stuffed parathas when Kashvi entered the kitchen.

"Wow, aloo paratha, how the boring poha is replaced with paratha today?" Her mother stared at her and passed her the plate.

"What do you think, when would be the ideal month to meet Praneel's family?" Mrs. Sharma questioned.

"Give us a few more months, don't rush," she replied sternly.

"Is everything ok?" her mom questioned.

"Yes, all good," she answered.

"Will you come with me, or do you have different plans?"

"You go ahead; I will go to my office a little late today," Mrs. Sharma answered.

She reached her office and found Sarika eagerly waiting for her.

"Shall we go for a tea?" Sarika asked Kashvi. To her astonishment, Kashvi, who was usually reluctant to take an untimely break, agreed immediately that day.

"Oh, looks like I am going to hear a lot of sizzling stuff today." Sarika giggled playfully.

Kashvi gave a light laugh.

They both bought tea and found a corner table to talk without much disturbance.

"Tell me, had he called yesterday, or had you called?" Sarika was eager to hear from her friend, and, more importantly, she wanted to know whether Kashvi had clarified everything on her end.

"Yes," Kashvi responded, recounting everything to Sarika about the previous night's conversation with Praneel.

"Stop giving that stupid gape," she said stiffly.

"Stupid gape? I just witnessed the inception of a love story.

You are worried about my gaze," Sarika cleared her throat.

Kashvi smiled and asked, "I hope I did it right."

"Yes, absolutely, I told you from day one that he is a perfect guy, not because he is handsome and charming, but because I could see the honesty and love for you in his eyes. I am so happy for you, Kashvi."

"Don't start it again. Sarika."

"I will, said Sarika, folding her legs and sitting like a sage on the chair. (Sarika loved acting, and she did that often to tease her friend by changing her tone of voice, making odd gestures, acting like an old sage.)

"Please don't take it lightly, my child. The journey has begun. You are so reserved and have set up too many boundaries when it comes to building relationships, so it is not easy for anyone to get close to you. But you need to break that now." Sarika spoke in a fake heavy voice.

"Oh, God! Why did I agree to come on break with you?" Kashvi held her forehead.

"Every person is different, and you cannot expect them to behave like you." Sarika winked and continued.

"You don't express much to me, but I still understand your intentions because I have magical power. But you need to express certain things with Praneel. Now, don't take that for granted." Sarika explained to her friend, acting like a wise, old sage.

"Absolutely, Guruji! What more would you like to suggest?" Kashvi responded, keeping her cup aside.

"Talk, express, and live your life to the fullest." Sarika sprinkled a few drops of water on Kashvi using a glass on the table.

"Stop it now."

They enjoyed their tea with the extended, regular banters and then went back to their desks for work.

While leaving the office, Kashvi stopped Sarika.

"For so many days, I wanted to talk to you, but you are so clever that you always engage me in other idle discussions. Have you talked about your boyfriend to your parents?"

Sarika shook her head.

"Why? You were about to talk a few weeks back. Why are you delaying it now? Is everything okay?" Kashvi asked in a concerned voice.

"All good, but I am not sure if this is the right time to introduce him to my family," she replied.

"But why?" asked Kashvi.

"I told you, I can read people's minds, like I read Praneel's mind," she answered while wearing her sunglasses.

Kashvi snatched her sunglasses. "You always have an implausible excuse. Please don't give me this reason. After dating for a year, you realized it now. Hope you don't hurt someone in this. I hate this." Kashvi sputtered.

"Relax, nobody will get hurt. It is love, not a war." Sarika replied with a mischievous chuckle and took her sunglasses back from Kashvi's hand.

"You have a bigger project to focus on, don't stress yourself too much on these petty things. I want the meeting minutes at 9 AM sharp tomorrow," she smirked.

"What is that?" Kashvi asked.

"Project Praneel," she laughed and accelerated her bike, leaving the office parking space. It was time for their 'after-work race', the ritual they had followed since their college days—the bike race, which helped them regain their energy after a tiring day. Kashvi keyed in to start her bike and chased her. The road was vast and empty. Kashvi sped up and overtook Sarika, but Sarika entered a lane on the left that was a shortcut to her house. Kashvi slowed down, halted, and looked back.

On the way home, Kashvi sensed that Sarika was hiding something from her. She knew every move of her friend and how cautiously Sarika had masked the truth behind the sunglasses. The lane ahead was not the regular road to her house. Her thoughts raced, competing between the bike race and the question of not introducing her boyfriend to her parents.

She tried apprehending while parking her bike and stepped inside her house, wearing a worried look.

Turning on the music, she decided to demystify the lingering question that had been on her mind and made a call to her friend. The call couldn't connect, and she heard only a busy signal. "She must be catching up with her boyfriend. Why am I intruding on her time? I assume everyone else lives their life as I do. Like always,

I am over-analyzing." She smiled inwardly, joining the clues and acknowledging what her friend had shared with her in the office.

Her gaze settled upon her mother, who was engrossed in scanning her bank passbook.

"Are you checking your bank balance? Will it be sufficient to spend on lavish and unnecessary arrangements for my wedding?" She peeked into the passbook.

Mrs. Sharma clearly looked unimpressed and noted down some figures on paper, which she carefully folded and kept in an envelope.

"You can wrap the paper, but I have not wrapped up my inquiry yet," Kashvi added.

"The envelope is sealed, so you should do the same with your mouth," Mrs. Sharma ended the conversation.

"There is a farewell invitation from one of my colleagues." Kashvi lifted her eyebrows questioningly.

"Get ready; we will leave in a little while." Mrs. Sharma completed her sentence.

By the time they returned home, it was nine. Kashvi quickly unlocked the door and parked the bike. Her mother had already climbed up, so she rushed to change her dress and, in a few minutes, she was in her room. It was 9:20 PM, but there was no call from Praneel yet.

She checked the message box to see if there was any message from him. There were no messages in the inbox. She was a little worried thinking about last night's wrangle with Praneel.

"What if he is still angry and has changed his mind?" With each passing minute, the tension rose, and the nervousness kicked in. She waited a little longer, then picked up her book to read. She kept checking her phone every few minutes, but didn't call him.

At last, her phone rang at around 10:46 PM, and her eyes were beaming with joy.

She answered the call.

"You didn't sleep today, you sound quite awake," inquired Praneel.

"Yes, I wanted to, but I was waiting for your call."

"For my call for...?" he asked playfully. She did not reply to his question.

"Do you know, you only wait for someone's call when you are in ...", he said in a gentle tone and paused briefly.

"When are you in?" She questioned in an uneasy, reserved voice.

"When you are in a queue, and the number you are trying to call is not reachable. Stupid," he chided, but full of fondness.

A smile tugged at her lips with a sense of achievement by dissolving a romantic moment into casual banter.

'Kashvi, I am sorry.'

'Sorry about?'

"About yesterday, I think I overreacted. Sometimes I struggle to control my anger. That's something I need to fix."

"It is okay as long as you are aware and working on it. It is a common problem. People overreact in anger."

"And, you scared me when you went quiet." He twisted the conversation with a light jest.

After a few minutes of nattering, there was a pause, and this time Praneel laughed to break the silence.

"Why are you laughing?" she asked.

"I was waiting for this moment."

"What does 'this moment' mean here?" she asked.

"The Pause," and he laughed again. Praneel continued to discuss his plans to move forward in his career and asked the same of Kashvi. They discussed some missed opportunities and then continued with their usual talks.

This had become a part of their daily life now. He used to call her twice or thrice a day — quick calls in the morning, at noon, and in the evening were just to check how she was doing, which still ended in less than five minutes.

The most awaited and important call at night used to be the last call of their day. This continued for days, weeks, and months. They discussed their childhood and college days, their likes and dislikes, memorable events, exchanged secrets, and shared funny stories about their family, friends, and relatives.

A night after a long exchange of words, when Kashvi was about to hang up the call.

"Do you mind if I ask something?"

She was bemused because he had always put her on the spot by asking questions.

"Do you love me?" he asked.

She was blank, umm, and there was stillness in the room.

He smiled and sensed the awkwardness in the silence, and said, "Leave this, tell me, when should we get married? I mean by the end of this year or next year?"

She was blank again. "Ahh, not sure. Moreover, both families have to decide, too."

"No," he laughed. "We have to decide and inform them."

"Oh, ok," she sounded dismayed.

"Now, reply. You cannot skip this question," he indicated again.

"Any time is fine," there was resentment in her response.

"Why do you sound so abashed? I was asking, so I can plan certain things on my end. Let us talk tomorrow about this." The phone got disconnected before he could complete his sentence.

After abruptly ending the call, Kashvi did not feel well. She often felt too modest and unsure to react whenever someone asked her about the marriage plans or the date.

"I was never so indecisive about anything in my life, so why am I so uncertain about this most significant decision of my life?" As she experienced this again, discomfort crept in for not answering him.

Praneel had sensed that Kashvi was unhappy and angry, so he called her back.

"What happened?" He asked with concern.

"Nothing," she replied, hiding her uneasiness.

"It was not a big question. I asked if you had given it any thought. Tell me, what is bothering you?" He asked.

Kashvi was quiet, as expected, and Praneel continued.

"I was sure that I wouldn't get any answer from you."

"I have an answer for everything," she interrupted.

"I had thought about it several times, much before you would have thought."

"Then, answer, what is the problem?" asked Praneel.

"I am worried about leaving my mother alone after our marriage. I have to make some arrangements for my mother here so that she doesn't face any problems in my absence. What if there is an emergency? Who will be her support system here?"

After a brief moment of quiescence, she resumed, "If I don't reply or share my views immediately, that doesn't mean I would not have thought about it." She expressed her concerns in a stern voice.

"You need to talk about it. There is a solution to it. I know that after your father, you have supported your mother through good and bad times; you are an independent person and capable of managing everything, but you can share your problem with me now. I am there to support you with all these things. Why do you want to take the burden of everything?"

Kashvi wanted to interject during his lengthy sermon, but after listening to him today, she felt relieved. She realized she has someone she can rely on. She had gotten rid of a burden, which she had been carrying for so many days. Over time, she realized that they had built a strong emotional connection, which was comforting. Apart from her mother, she had a close bond with someone, and she was no longer alone.

He continued his spiel, "If nothing works, she can shift to the same city wherever we will settle down after marriage. Do you foresee any other problem?" He asked.

"No," Kashvi replied in a dull tone.

"There is a solution to every problem. It is up to us whether we want to accept it or not. If you cannot accept the solution, then accept the problem and live with it," he said.

It is a beautiful feeling when you know you have someone you can rely on, who will hold your hand through thick and thin and give you unwavering support to walk the lifelong journey.

Apart from all this, she also liked how he outsmarted her, a quality she always admired in Praneel.

Praneel was aware of her mother's struggle after her father's untimely demise. He acknowledged and valued Kashvi's ability to manage things single-handedly without complaining or drawing anyone's attention to it. Another impressive quality that he adored in Kashvi as a companion.

"You are not alone now. There is someone who cares for you, and you matter to me more than anyone else," he added warmly.

He took a deep breath and changed the topic to something light yet romantic. "By the way, you wisely skipped my first question and straightaway jumped to the other question."

"What does that mean?" With a bundle of worries and in a rage, she had forgotten what Praneel had asked her before inquiring about the marriage date.

"You just mentioned that you have answers to all my questions. Then, give an elaborate answer to my first question," he asked impishly.

Kashvi recalled his first question and hesitated again, but she did not want to appear dubious at this point and answered, "Of course, yes. If not, why would I be wasting my time on these calls for the past so many months?" She replied bluntly.

Praneel laughed uncontrollably and suggested that she could have answered it differently with a pinch of love.

"Good night!" said Kashvi.

"Hold up for a bit. I will never ask anything to make you feel small. I will never be the reason for your sadness. Keep this in mind. Good night, sleep tight!" Praneel playfully added. The call got disconnected.

Kashvi prepared her bed for sleep; she knew that soon she would receive a message from Praneel. The phone buzzed. Kashvi opened the message and read, "I love you!" Her heart pounded after reading the message. She replied with a smiley :)

VII

Love is in the Air

————•♡•————

Love stories can have happy or sad endings, but the morning after the confession of love is always enchanting. Seeing someone accept your proposal makes the day even more splendid and gratifying. That is the magic of love, which you experience only once in your life.

Love is never about a wealthy partner, a luxury lifestyle, the exchange of grand gifts, or external appearance. Arguments and disagreements are part of life, but true love lies in mutual understanding, supporting your partner, caring for each other, finding joy in little things, and standing together in tough times.

This morning was unrivaled for both Kashvi and Praneel.

Kashvi was extremely happy, and the joyous feeling was ineffable. She pushed the curtains aside, walked toward the balcony, and placidly watched the beautiful sun rays falling on the dew drops that were hanging from the blades of leaves.

His words echoed in her ears, and she tickled pink.

The flowering plants brushed against each other with the gush of air; a tiny bird landed on the lawn and flitted in the small puddle formed in the corner of the garden. The bird kept splashing the water until it was completely drenched.

The composed morning did not last for long when the news-hawker entered the street and started ringing its cycle bell. The 'ding-dong' sound approached closer; he rolled and threw the newspaper in the air, navigating it toward the balcony. The thumping sound flew the bird away. She took the newspaper and rushed inside to get ready for her office.

It was a blissful morning for Praneel, but it soon became busy when he stepped out for his office. The street was bustling with people, and while driving his car toward his office, he got stuck in traffic. He never liked to be stuck in morning traffic, but he was amazed that he did not lose his temper today. The song that he had played in the car was pleasing to the ear and reminded him of Kashvi. Her mere thought kept him delighted throughout the day. Looking at the traffic that was moving at a snail's pace, he took the opportunity to give a call to Kashvi.

While she was working, her phone rang.

She disconnected and replied through a message.

I am busy with some work. Give me some time.

What is 'some time' equal to? He texted.

I am not sure, maybe after 30 minutes. She texted back.

Alright, I will wait. He texted back.

Sarika caught a glimpse of Kashvi and, as usual, started teasing her for being happy and smiling throughout the day.

She got a call promptly after 30 minutes. She wanted to answer the call this time, but her manager had summoned the team for an ad hoc meeting, which, according to him, should not exceed 10 minutes. So, she texted Praneel: Got into an urgent meeting. I will call you in 15 minutes.

Praneel texted back. That is not fair. You said 30 minutes, and now you're adding 15 more.

She answered with a smiley. The meeting ended. She quickly grabbed her phone and went outside to call him back. She was about to dial his number when suddenly her phone rang. She answered in a hasty tone.

"Hello, sorry, I was about to call you, but this meeting got extended."

"That's okay. Tell me, have you seen the message I sent last night?" Praneel interrupted.

"Oh, yes, I replied, too," she answered hurriedly.

"What was the message?" Praneel asked wittily.

"I know which message you are referring to. I saw and replied to it too," Kashvi answered overtly.

"No, you didn't answer my message," said Praneel.

"I had sent a smiley," Kashvi countered.

"Yes, exactly, and a smiley is not an answer. Tell me, will you reply now?"

Praneel teased her with his usual playful and friendly remarks for not expressing her feelings for him. When he felt he had teased her enough for the day, he gave her an option.

"Let me make it easy for you. You can text me."

"Is that why you were calling me?" asked Kashvi.

"Yes, of course, what else were you expecting?"

"I saw that emoticon and had a sleepless night. Anticipating that you will reply, I waited in the morning too." He sighed.

"Can we talk later? I have some work to finish." She spoke.

"Ok, no problem. I will wait for your reply."

The day in the office flew by with back-to-back meetings. It was 6:30 PM, time to go back home. Sarika had already left as she had some personal work. Kashvi went down to the parking space and was about to leave when her phone rang again.

"I am still waiting," he said.

"What? I am still in the office and have not reached home yet," she replied.

"So, will you reply after reaching home?" he continued teasing her.

"Yes," she quickly answered to get rid of his question. "Don't you have any work in your office today?" she asked.

"I have, but I cannot work. Every time I try to focus, I see you," he replied playfully.

"What? Crazy!" she replied, hiding her smile. "Go, take a break. You will be fine," she suggested.

"Yes, I need a break. You are right," he paused and replied. "I want to meet you." Kashvi's heart was beating fast, and she was thinking, what is he going to say now?

"It is getting late. I will call you after reaching home."

"And you never do that," he complained.

"Bye," she replied and then disconnected the call.

After reaching home, she was worried whether he would ask her to respond to the message again. How would she answer? She took a sly look in the kitchen and could smell the boiling tea on the gas stove. Her book lay on the corner table, which she picked up to read, and started flipping through the pages, and was preoccupied with Praneel's question. Mrs. Sharma placed two cups of tea with some snacks on the coffee table.

"Mrs. Tripathi had called in the afternoon," she paused. Kashvi paid attention, raising her eyebrows, and the cup lingered near her lips. A faint crease on Mrs. Sharma's face made her inquisitive and anxious at the same time.

"Mrs. Tripathi often talks about one proposal she preferred, but Praneel had rejected. She also steered the discussion toward marriage arrangements today, which is fine, but the latter puzzles me."

Kashvi took a sip and leaned back, "Hmm, she is trying to convey a message, which you are unable to comprehend."

Mrs. Sharma intriguingly stared at her, listening to her response.

"You really don't understand what I am trying to tell?" Kashvi smiled. The phone rang again. She knew it must be Praneel's call.

"Why are you not picking up the call?" Mrs. Sharma questioned.

"Let me have some tea and take a rest," she replied.

"At least tell him that you will call later. Why don't you pick up and talk to him?" She questioned again.

Listening to her mother's mandatory advice, Kashvi was clearly annoyed, but she controlled her reaction.

"Oh, I would..." and before she could complete the sentence, her mom picked up the phone. Kashvi was even more worried now. What if he says something to her mom, thinking it is Kashvi on the call?

Praneel was about to open his mouth, but upon hearing her mother's voice, he quickly changed his response.

"Hello, Aunty. How are you?" he asked decently.

"All good. Is everything fine at your end?"

"Yes, Aunty," he replied.

I spoke with your mother today. She informed me about a few customs and rituals that are followed in your family, and umm, she paused. The urge to inquire about the proposal Mrs. Tripathi mentioned on the call was about to flow, but she resisted and changed the topic.

"Praneel, is there something important? Kashvi is having tea, and she will call you back after sometime."

"Why do you need to tell all these things?" Kashvi looked at her mom and muttered.

"That's fine. I had called to check if she got any message from the company where she had applied for the job," he said carefully.

"Oh, has she? She did not inform me."

Kashvi started thinking about what he had been talking to her mother about.

"Maybe she is waiting for the confirmation and then wants to share the news with you. No issues, let her take a rest. I will call at night," and he disconnected the call.

Soon after the call ended, her mother asked, "Kashvi, have you applied for a job?"

Kashvi was bemused, thinking, "What is that?" Then she realized that a few days back, she had applied through a job portal.

"Yes, I had, but I have not received any response yet," she replied to her mother's question.

Praneel was asking about it.

She took a deep breath and figured out what story he had made up now. Mrs. Sharma went out with Kashvi to buy some groceries. Kashvi received a message from Praneel.

The wait is pretty long.

I am going out and will call at night, she texted back.

Oh, are you waiting for the right time? He texted and added a winking emoji.

Keep waiting, she replied with a growling emoticon.

Both mother and daughter meandered across the streets. At last, Kashvi stopped on one side of the road, while her mother continued scanning and inspecting vegetables from all the vendors in that busy lane, where you cannot stop without bumping into someone. She kept bargaining with vegetable vendors to get the best deal. She returned with a bag full of green leafy vegetables and was glad to have won the best deal, which hardly saved her 12 Rupees.

"By the way, Ma, what was the discussion between you and Aunty, which you left incomplete over the tea?"

"Oh, yes." Mrs. Sharma took a deep breath. "I feel Mrs. Tripathi had chosen another girl for Praneel, which he didn't like, and she still believes that girl is well suited for her son."

With a sudden jerk, the bike stopped.

"Careful! I mean, she doesn't say that directly; however, I can sense what she was trying to say." Mrs. Sharma shared her opinion.

"Okay, and what was the other topic?" Kashvi posed the question carefully.

"They come from a prominent and reputable family, and everybody is wealthy. She was inquiring if we would be able to spend enough to match their status."

"Ma, and you chose to share all this now." She said while parking her bike.

"Before talking about marriage arrangements and expenses, I think you should not forget about that meeting." She reminded her mother about their upcoming meeting with his parents, adding sharply.

"I really hope none of these things turn up as a massive shock to us when we all meet in Indore." Her mother glossed over her statement and climbed up the stairs.

The clock struck nine. Kashvi knew she could no longer run away and had to answer Praneel now. She was scratching her head to find a solution to avoid his question, but she could not find a better answer. Moreover, the conversation she had with her mother was swirling in her head. After spending hours, she decided to discuss and clear up any confusion regarding their marriage. **She knew these elders would talk about everything except what was really important.**

The phone rang at 9:20 PM. She answered with ambivalence and heard Praneel laughing on the other end of the phone. She became even more cautious.

"What happened? Why are you laughing?"

"I am laughing at you," he answered.

"Why?" she asked.

"You know the answer. You have just been trying to escape from me since this morning," said Praneel.

"Nothing like that, I was busy," she answered awkwardly.

"Really?" he asked.

"Yes."

"What was that big thing you were busy with? Can you tell me?" he scorned.

Kashvi was quiet, but then answered smartly.

"I was browsing through different job openings in Hyderabad and applying for them."

"Oh yes, tell me, have you got any call?" he asked anxiously.

"Yes, I got a few, but for the initial rounds. It will take some time as they prefer candidates from the same city."

"Yes, you are right. Keep trying; you never know when it strikes."

When Praneel was busy explaining to her about the companies, the recruitment process, and what else she could change on her résumé, Kashvi was glad that she had successfully diverted Praneel and saved herself from answering Praneel's message from the previous night.

"The only obstacle that I see is that you cannot apply for frequent leaves to attend multiple rounds of interviews. In addition, traveling from one city to another would be a problem. As a result, it will be difficult for you to find a job. Perhaps if you crack the interview at the first company, then there won't be any problem," said Praneel.

"Anyway, there is no hurry, we have enough time," Kashvi replied, and regretted it at the same time. With this statement, she closed the confab and set the stage for Praneel to return to the previous topic.

"Yes, you are right, we have time. If you can take a whole day to reply to my message, then certainly, you have ample time," Praneel mocked again.

"You are so boring, Kashvi."

"Yes, I am," she acknowledged with a firm voice.

"I am still waiting for your reply, and I won't hang up the call till I get my answer," he remarked.

"I don't know if I can reply or not. If you want to wait, then wait," Kashvi said in her discomfited voice.

Praneel laughed again and asked, "Do you love me?" "Yes," she replied guardedly.

"That's it. Was it so difficult?"

"You shy away from expressing yourself when you like someone. You hesitate to answer simple questions when you are falling for someone. You tolerate the playful taunts when they matter to you. **And** ... you wait for someone when you are in love.

His words were full of affection that left her spellbound.

Hold on for a few minutes, I will come back," said Praneel. She liked how Praneel always made things easy for her.

"Are you there?" he asked.

"Yes."

"Listen to this song, this one's for you," he said.

Kashvi paid attention to the music; Praneel had played a romantic song for her. The song stopped, and she blushed.

"I have been listening to it since morning. He confessed warmly. Hope you like it."

"Yes, it is a melodious song," she replied.

Their call continued. The conversation was filled with teasing and laughter. In the middle of that playful banter, her mind urged her to bring up that critical topic, but her heart resisted. She could sense the joy and excitement in his voice, which she didn't want to spoil.

The call ended, and she received a message from Praneel: With every beat of my heart, my love for you is becoming stronger. I love you.

Kashvi replied to his message with a smiley.

VIII
The Interview

Day after day rolled on, and Kashvi had started looking for a job in Hyderabad, where Praneel lived. After some meaningful exchanges with Praneel on the call, she realized the importance of planning ahead. Life changes after marriage: new family, new members, a different routine, and on top of that, she has to juggle two new roles and responsibilities in her life simultaneously—one at home as Praneel's life partner and the other at the workplace as a new employee. They discussed and decided that it would be good if she could take up a new job at a new company a little before their marriage; it would make things easier and more manageable, especially for Kashvi.

In the past few months, while talking to Kashvi, Praneel was enthralled to find a life partner who understands him and values his opinions, who stands by his side as a true companion.

He doesn't want to marry a girl who agrees to everything he says and is dependent on him. He always wanted someone he could depend on for the crucial decisions of his life, whom he felt he found in Kashvi.

At times, he used to get jittery because of her impassive responses, especially when it was about expressing her love for him. But after listening to her simple, mature, and responsible talk, this fear had also mellowed.

One morning, she did not wake to an alarm. It was Praneel's call. She looked at the time flashing on the screen and struggled to open her eyes. She brought the phone to her ear and responded to the call.

Good morning, Kashvi!

"Morning, Praneel. What happened?" she replied in a quavering voice.

"Are you sleeping?" he asked.

She looked at the screen again, baffled at his question. It was 6:00 AM. "Yes, what should I be doing then at this time?"

"Rise and shine, gorgeous. You have an interview tomorrow," his voice rustled through the phone. She was wide awake now.

"And how do you know?"

"I had referred you to my friend's company, and he informed me that they will schedule an interview tomorrow over a call. You will receive an email today. Now, get up fast and plan to crack it. I am eager to meet you."

His voice sounded warm as always; she smiled and disconnected the call.

She informed her mother about Praneel's call and her interview at the breakfast table. Mrs. Sharma was happy to hear the news, but Kashvi could see a hidden, dull feeling behind her subtle smile.

"What happened, ma?"

"Nothing! Prepare well for your interview and try to grab this opportunity as soon as possible. Never forget that marriage comes with a huge responsibility, and enjoy that journey with your life partner by taking care of your family."

It had been months since her marriage was fixed with Praneel, and Mrs. Sharma had never said anything like that to her. Whatever her mother said made sense, but her last few words stung, and she realized that soon she would be living far from her mother—the feeling she did not want to experience.

They both silently had their breakfast and left for their office. That day, when Kashvi dropped her mother at the gate of her office, she felt a surge of emotion and did not look back, but raced her bike toward her office.

"Everything piles up at the same time." She spoke, checking on her emails.

When she opened her personal mailbox, she found an email from the company's recruitment staff that Praneel had mentioned on the morning call. She filled in the required details on the form and attached her résumé.

When she was looking at the screen to click the send button, Sarika called her for a break. She had noticed Kashvi applying for a new job. Kashvi hit the send button in a bit of a rush. She followed Sarika to grab a cup of coffee, which she had been eagerly waiting for. She had so many questions on her mind.

"Sarika, is this the right time to get married, or should I wait a little longer?"

"From where is this coming from?" Sarika was baffled by her questions.

"I am thinking about Mom."

"You are doing the right thing. Our mothers, too, have left their parents, so don't think too much."

She knew her friend's state of mind, so she knew the words she had to pick up to soothe her anxious friend, muddling around the complex circle of queries for leaving her mother alone in this city.

While they were conversing, she got a call from Praneel. As the number flashed on her mobile screen, Sarika teased her again.

"Come on, Kashvi, you cannot be in this dilemma now. Look at this guy; he is waiting for you to spend the rest of his life with you." She realized her friend was right and picked up his call.

"Have you received the email?" He asked curiously.

"Yes, and I have applied for it. I don't think the interview will be conducted tomorrow; almost half a day has gone by, and I have submitted the details now. So, it will take time to process," clarified Kashvi.

"That is fine, you be prepared, it is up to them when they want to conduct," said Praneel.

It was an overwhelming day for Kashvi, both at work and emotionally. She reached home and spent the whole evening talking to her mother.

Once in a blue moon, Kashvi would spend more time talking rather than reading books. Her mother observed this shift, but she resisted questioning the reason behind the change in her mundane routine. She understood that Kashvi was apprehensive about being away from her mother.

Within a few days, the interview got scheduled. Kashvi had cleared her initial rounds of the interview, and the company had invited her for the final round in Hyderabad. They wanted to conduct the final round in-person.

Kashvi shared this news with Mrs. Sharma, and she was worried about her daughter traveling to that city alone. She informed her mother not to worry, as she would return in a day or so after the interview. Praneel had informed his parents about Kashvi visiting Hyderabad for her interview. As the only son, Praneel was always doted on at home. He was a free-spirited guy and would often inform his parents about his plans without seeking their permission. It had become difficult for his parents when he refused to marry any of the girls they suggested. They were happy with the news that soon their son would get settled, and as planned, things were gradually moving in their son's life.

Kashvi had booked an early-morning flight, and her interview was scheduled after 12 PM, which she felt would be manageable in case there was a travel delay.

Praneel was desperately waiting for Kashvi at the airport. The flight landed on time, and when she stepped out of the arrival gate, she found Praneel waiting for her right in front of it, one hand in his pocket and the other holding his mobile. Looking at her adorable smile and dazzling eyes, he felt his heart beat faster. She looked elegant and pretty in her light pink cotton kurta and churidar.

As she walked closer to him in her heels, he was captivated and lost in the moment. They both looked at each other and smiled. His eyes locked with Kashvi's eyes, and when Praneel did not look away from her, she looked away from him and asked, "How long has he been waiting here?"

"An hour or so," he answered, and extended his hand to offer her help in carrying her bag.

"I can manage," she replied and looked at the café behind him.

"Can we go and have coffee before we start from here?" she asked.

"Of course, what would you like to have?"

Praneel had thoughtfully planned her visit because he wanted to meet Kashvi, and he could not find any other way to meet her. Being aware of Kashvi's reserved attitude, he also knew that if he ever asked to meet her, she would not have agreed, so he had kept his plans hidden from her. One of his friends in the recruitment department had helped him arrange an in-person meeting for the last round of the interview.

While she was settling herself in the coffee shop, Praneel went and ordered two cups of coffee and sandwiches. The coffee and sandwiches were quickly served at their table, and while she took a sip of her coffee, he asked, "You did that intentionally."

"What?" she asked.

"You diverted me when I was lost in your eyes," he said mischievously. She was scrolling through her phone to call her mother and smiled as she listened to his response.

"Where did you learn all these lines?" She asked, dialing her mother.

"Yes, I landed safely."

"Have you met Praneel?"

"Yes, and right now he is staring, I mean, he is sitting

in front of me," she replied, looking at Praneel.

Kashvi looked agitated now. Praneel smiled, adjusted himself, and determined not to do anything stupid now.

"I will call you before boarding the flight," her mother wished her luck for her interview, and she hung up the call, saying thanks!

"You can help me with the route and then go back to your office," suggested Kashvi.

"I have taken leave today, and I will drive you to the office."

"Oh, I could have managed to get to that office; I kept enough time in my hand, too."

"I know, you can manage everything by pointing at her bag. It is a long drive, and I wanted to spend this time with you," Praneel looked at her and smiled.

They went to the parking area where Praneel had parked his car. He opened the door for Kashvi. When Kashvi sat inside, Praneel was delighted to have her next to him in his car. He noticed Kashvi was wearing the same bracelet.

"Will it not tangle up with your attire and tear it?" he quipped, pointing at the bracelet.

"No, it won't, I have fixed it." She tightened her lips, turned her face to the window, and recalled the statement she had made in their first meeting. They both exchanged glances, and the blushful silence burst into laughter.

He played his favorite song and mentioned that the music was dedicated to her.

Along the way, he shared his plans to settle in that city. He also mentioned the project that will keep him pretty busy in the coming months and how being associated with it would be beneficial in the long term. Kashvi paid attention to everything he shared and recommended several essential points that she felt would be a worthy addition for his quick career growth. It was a long drive, but with the back-and-forth conversation, they didn't realize how much time had passed. He dropped Kashvi at the main gate and waited at a restaurant a few yards away from the technology park.

It was almost two hours, so he messaged Kashvi— All good?

He did not get any reply. He waited a little longer and then called her.

"It went well, almost done. I will be out in a few minutes. Where are you?" She replied in a cheerful voice.

"Wait at the gate." Praneel advised.

Praneel drove back to the main gate. As he got down, she spoke about every aspect of the interview in a flow. She was excited to be selected, and her happiness glowed on her face.

"I have never heard you sound so enthusiastic about anything. More than you, I am glad that you don't have to put yourself in trouble by searching and applying for a job now," he said.

On the way, he pointed at the dashboard box and asked her to open it. A rolled paper, tied with a red satin ribbon, was lying in the corner of the box. She raised her eyebrows in question.

"Take it out and open it." He alluded to her.

She pulled it out and untied the ribbon. When she unrolled it, she was amazed to see her sketch, which was drawn on that paper.

Praneel observed that the usual slight smile was replaced with a broad smile on her face. "The artwork is captivating," she said and paused, "not because it is my picture, but the lines, thickness, and shading, everything is so detailed and fine. You had mentioned that you do sketching in your free time, but I was not aware of the level of proficiency you have in it."

"I love this," she said gleefully, staring at the art.

"And I love you," he added, turning the steering wheel.

"Impressive and profuse hospitality," she uttered in a sigh.

"Roll it and put it back," he instructed.

"Why? I thought it was a gift for me," she asked in a coltish manner.

"I wanted to cross-check if I had made any mistakes while drawing and putting my thoughts into it. It is a gift I gifted to myself," he dotingly replied, looking at the road ahead.

She carefully rolled the paper, tied it, and kept it back with a contented smile. The sun, at the horizon, was getting ready to set, and the rays were penetrating through the front glass. Her face still looking stunning, he watched in the rearview mirror of his car.

"Can we have a coffee before you rush inside the airport for check-in?" Praneel expressed his wish after parking his car.

"Yes."

They walked together to a coffee shop with an open space, making the seating area airy and spacious. High chairs and wooden furniture were placed, creating an inviting ambience. As the sun was about to set, the evening had become pleasant and perfect to sip piping hot coffee. They found a cozy place and settled themselves. In no time, the coffee was served at their table.

"Look at the colors, it is the golden hour," she said, looking at the sky.

"It was a golden day for me," Praneel answered, looking at her. I had been waiting for this day for a long time. A talk, a chat, a discussion, a conversation of any kind, everything just fit in so easily and perfectly with you. Taking a deep breath, he continued—All my worries diminish when I am with you. A sense of ease, or I should rather say being with you, makes me feel complete, he revealed tenderly. His eyes were still steady on her.

"I couldn't get time to explore this city," she added, "and you kept me engaged in your talks that I couldn't even notice the route you took to reach the airport," she said.

"Kashvi, don't you feel like calling and talking to me?"

"No." Kashvi's response left him speechless.

"You never give me a chance, Praneel."

"In the old days, people never had this option," she pointed at her mobile, "and still their love and commitment to their loved ones were far more profound and stronger than you see between couples in these times. Call someone, talk to them frequently, message them. Why do we need these validations to prove ourselves continually to someone?"

He was astounded listening to her.

"Not everything can be expressed in words; sometimes, the unspoken expressions and being available for your dear ones in crucial times are the purest form of love. For some reason, if you cannot call me for a few days, does that mean that you don't love me anymore? If I don't call you, does that mean that I don't love you?"

His lips tightened as he listened to her.

"Can I ask something, Praneel? He looked at her in silent amazement.

"Does aunty have someone else in mind for you?" She had not planned to, but she finally brought up the unresolved riddle she had always refrained from asking Praneel.

"What's that? Has she said anything to you?"

"Not to me. This was brought up in the conversation a couple of times with mom, so I thought I would clear up any ambiguities around it." She spoke, stirring her coffee.

"Yes, she preferred another girl, someone known from her friend's circle, but I had made it clear to her long ago. He gently took her hand and elaborated. All this happened almost two years ago. A lot of arguments were made about this. That topic has been dead. I don't know why she has to talk about it now. I will speak to her."

"Not required. Let us put an end to this topic." She replied with a soft smile.

"Kashvi, I have told my parents clearly that I want to marry you."

"I didn't ask for clarification. She smiled and concluded the conversation.

"It is time to leave now," she said while taking out her card to make a payment. Praneel stopped her and handed the change at the counter. They walked in silence toward the entrance gate.

"It is not easy for everyone to express their feelings. Don't misinterpret me if I don't call you frequently. In the toughest times, you will always find me beside you. She added warmly, placing her bag on the ground.

"You make my heart skip every time with your responses. He took her hand and spoke in a lowered voice. She slowly pulled her hand away and smiled.

Praneel laughed at her gesture.

"You wait for a few more months, and I will never let it go again," he replied in an affectionate voice.

She laughed lightly and then quickly paced to enter the airport.

IX
The Meeting Again

A few months passed, and the date had been set for the pre-wedding ritual, when Kashvi's and Praneel's families would meet to make this relationship official. Both families decided to meet in winter, as it had been almost a year now. None of them wanted to delay the wedding plans further.

The meeting was delayed because Praneel was on an official tour and at the client's place, working on a critical project.

'It is difficult for me to take leave until the end of December, Ma.'

'I don't know anything. After so much calculation, Panditji could see only a favorable date in the first week of December. If you cannot come, your father and I can meet them and exchange Shagun.' Mrs. Tripathi said.

She was superstitious about the date and time, which had been informed by a well-known and learned family priest whom she believed and followed blindly.

According to their priest, the auspicious date fell in the first week of the month, and she wanted to meet Kashvi during that specific time period to finalize the wedding dates. Praneel tried to persuade her to wait a few more weeks, but Mrs. Tripathi was firm in her belief. According to her, she could meet Kashvi and her family and perform a small ritual to confirm the dates. In the end, they all agreed to meet in Praneel's absence.

ϼϼϼ

"I am thrilled," there was an excitement in Praneel's voice.

"Yeah," Kashvi sighed.

"Aren't you?" questioned Praneel.

"I am," she replied hesitantly.

"What happened?"

"What if they say no?" she asked.

Praneel was startled by her question and asked anxiously, "And why do you think so? They are going to meet you and your family to do the pre-wedding ritual. Now, it is not about saying yes or no."

"Hold on, was there any such palaver between you and my family?" Praneel questioned again, thinking something had happened that he was not aware of.

"No, nothing happened."

"Then, why are you overthinking?"

"It was just a thought that popped up, and I asked."

"Thoughts only pop up when they are seeded. They only expand their roots in the mind when something around us helps in nurturing and growing them," lectured Praneel.

Kashvi knew she now had to explain everything to him, which she hated to do again. She muttered "yes" in agreement, barely audible.

"You know, I don't like it when you give half answers," said Praneel, cutting her off in the middle.

"Are you going to tell me now, or do you need 30-40 minutes of an open-ended session again?" he said darkly.

Finally, she poured her heart out and revealed her concerns she had been holding back since the day her mother told her about their meeting with his parents.

"In Indian society, people are obsessed with light skin tone, especially when it comes to their daughter-in-law."

"Really, and you, being an educated girl, believe all this nonsense," mocked Praneel.

"Haven't you seen matrimonial advertisements? Looking for a bride, a fair girl ..."

"Has anything happened recently, Kashvi?

"No, but I am aware of the societal pressure and how people in society prefer a fair-skinned daughter-in-law and a perfect match for their son."

"I don't know about others, but I know my parents. Their thoughts are not so condescending. I have no idea what made you think all this."

"I have seen this happening now and then in society," she replied in a firm and agitated tone.

"See, Kashvi, you look gorgeous to me. I am not in India now, and I don't know what is happening at your end. Who is watering such notions in your head?"

There was silence for a while.

"For me, you are the most beautiful girl I have ever met, and I want to spend my life with you," Praneel replied in a stern voice.

Kashvi struggled to find the right words to explain the situation that might arise after meeting his parents. It can be a whole different scenario. Furthermore, she also wanted to know how Praneel would deal with it.

"Parents' expectations are different from ours. They always want a perfect partner for their children. I am not saying that somebody's preference is wrong or right, but when it is about their children, every parent wants to select the best in everything," clarified Kashvi.

"I don't want to debate. I know what I want in my life partner, and I have informed my parents about my choice. And I want you to stop thinking about something that has not happened and would never happen." He replied assertively.

"Have you packed everything for tomorrow's travel?" Praneel asked, changing the debate to candid exchanges.

"Yes," Kashvi whispered.

Though Praneel had spoken enough to convince Kashvi that she is the one he wants to spend his whole life with, his parents' opinion cannot change his decision. Kashvi still had the same dilemma. She pretended that she believed him. She tried to hide her feelings through her vague response. Praneel was familiar with her responses and understood Kashvi's state of mind.

"Tell me, what are you going to ask my parents?" he asked in a playful way to brighten her up.

Initially, she did not understand, but soon she realized he was pulling her leg.

"What do you mean?" she asked.

"You hosted me with countless indirect questions to draw all the required information when I met you for the first time. Won't you ask a few questions to my parents?" he quipped again.

She did not say anything.

"I know you are still stuck on the same topic. Tell me, what should I say or do to dispel all the fears and doubts that you have built around yourself? Kashvi, I chose you because I love you," he reassured in a husky voice. "Everything will be fine."

"Yes," she sighed. In her mind, she had harbored the contentious issue and had decided to hold off until

Pandora's box opened.

"Can I ask something?" he asked.

"Yes, tell me."

"The bracelet you wore when we met, don't forget to wear it," he pointed out.

"Why?" she asked curiously.

"That's a lucky charm for me," he said quietly. They both laughed together.

The soulful chat continued, and Kashvi indicated that she had received an email from the company where she was interviewed last month. The company had put the position on hold for some reason.

"Don't worry, there are many companies where you can apply."

"Let me sleep now, we have an early morning train," said Kashvi.

"Hmm, message when you reach Indore. I will be busy at the client site. I won't be able to call you."

"That's okay."

"And smile. Everything will be fine." He assured her.

ppp

Kashvi and Mrs. Sharma reached Indore. Her parents' family belonged to the same city. Her father's younger brother (Raghu) had suggested this proposal for Kashvi. He had met Praneel's father at one of their distant relatives' gatherings. During the casual discussion, Mr. Tripathi mentioned that they were looking for a suitable match for their son, and soon Raghu Uncle briefed him about his niece, Kashvi.

Kashvi and her mother arrived at her uncle's place late at night. Her uncle (Raghu) and aunt (Neelam) were excited to see them.

"Bhabhi, if Dada is watching from the universe, he must be proud of me for keeping my promise," he said to Mrs. Sharma.

During their brief conversation, Kashvi noticed a sense of achievement on her uncle's face, as the proposal he had suggested was soon going to turn into a long-lasting relationship.

The following morning, the sound of the mantra reverberated throughout the house. It was Tuesday morning, and Raghu Uncle was reciting the Hanuman Chalisa; the fragrance of camphor spread through the rooms. It grew stronger when he entered Kashvi's room, holding the pooja plate. He was ringing the pooja bell with one hand and waving the pooja plate in a circular motion with the other. There was dim light in the room where she was sleeping, but as Raghu Uncle held the flame on the pooja plate, the room lit up. Kashvi instantly sat straight on her bed as she noticed her uncle taking rounds in the room.

"My devotional family—from Gwalior to Indore, I can never miss the morning bells, even God checks the time against their schedule." She smiled, attempting an elegant slouch against the headrest. She tried to settle down to take support and rest, but it was hard and uncomfortable.

She saw her uncle making his way out of the room and heard Neelam Aunty and her mother conversing over morning tea. They sounded lively even in the early morning dialogue. She was amused, harking back to their high-energy chatter at the crack of dawn.

"These ladies love to talk," she thought, and sluggishly climbed down the bed to wear her flip-flops.

Raghu Uncle brought the pooja plate in front of her; she hovered her hands over the lamp, placed her palms over her eyes, and then slowly raised them over her head to seek God's blessings. She yawned and dragged herself to the dining area, where Neelam Aunty and her mother were enjoying tea. She pulled out a chair and sat next to her aunt. Neelam Aunty was sipping tea and hastily chopping vegetables.

"Why are you cutting vegetables early in the morning? It is hardly 7 o'clock," Kashvi asked curiously.

"Have you forgotten Praneel's parents are visiting today?" she replied.

"Are they coming in the morning?" Kashvi asked.

"Of course not, they will be here by 3 PM. That is the auspicious time their priest suggested (she quipped about Mrs. Tripathi's faith), but we need to wrap up other regular chores on time.

There are so many arrangements that need to be done before they come," her aunt answered.

"What are the arrangements for? This is not an engagement." Kashvi intervened.

"You are right, this is not an engagement. This is a small ritual, or you can call it a custom, where families of a prospective bride and groom meet, exchange sweets and gifts, and formally announce that they have found the match for their daughter and son. After this, they share wedding dates with their relatives and friends," her aunt elaborated excitedly.

"Formal announcement," Kashvi repeated in amazement, and she whispered, "Was it not formal until now?"

"Let us have an early breakfast today," her aunt added. She transferred the chopped veggies from the chopping board to a plate using the edge of the knife and carried them into the kitchen.

Raghu Uncle had finished his prayers and was standing next to her with 'prasad' (offering).

Her uncle asked Mrs. Sharma to hand him the list of items that he needed to buy from the market.

He had to go and pick up the sweets and gifts from the big sweet mart.

"Hopefully, they have packed the boxes properly," he said while offering prasad to everyone in the house.

"Will many people be accompanying them?" Kashvi interrogated in a hushed voice.

"Not many, there will be only close family members," her uncle replied.

"Why are you worried?" he asked her.

"Not worried, just a question as you mentioned gifts and sweets," Kashvi replied warily.

"Whether it is small or big, everything will be done precisely and properly; after all, it is my niece's function," Raghu Uncle spoke in a delighted tone.

Kashvi smiled at her uncle's sweet gesture.

She looked at her mom's face; she looked worried.

"Is there any problem? You seem to be stressed out," she asked her mother.

"I am just worried. Will everything go well or not?" her mom replied.

"And why do you think so?" Although Kashvi had the same question, she asked for a few words of comfort.

"You never really know the guy's parents and what they expect. No matter how much you spend or how many arrangements you make, they always look for some flaw. It's hard to convince them," Mrs. Sharma sounded worried.

"Stop worrying, we are all here to look after everything. There won't be any challenges, and everything will go smoothly," Neelam Aunty shouted from the kitchen.

Since morning, there has been a lot of commotion in the house. Kashvi's father's elder brother (Viren) and his wife (Kiran) had also arrived by 9 AM. Everybody was busy making arrangements to ensure Praneel's family felt comfortable in the house. The house was looking vibrant with colorful curtains, bed sheets, and cushion covers. Kashvi noticed that all her uncles and aunts were working hard to make arrangements. Whenever she tried to pitch in to help them, they all suggested that she take a rest, as it was her day. Kashvi was happy and nervous at the same time.

There was a rush inside her house and in her heart, too.

The phone was continuously ringing at Tripathi's bungalow. The lawn in front of their house was neatly trimmed. Mr. Tripathi was on a call with Raghu ji, trying to get the address of their home. Raghu ji had mentioned every landmark along the way to their house. He had provided enough detail so that no one could get lost in the lanes and would, in fact, reach the destination on time.

"We will arrive at 3 PM." Mr. Tripathi replied.

Mr. Tripathi continued enjoying his tea with his younger brother (Sanjay) in the front yard.

"Praneel is a stubborn guy, and he has distanced himself from me," he complained to Sanjay, admiring his plants.

"How many times will you call, Praneel? Stop directing me, we will be there on time." Mrs. Tripathi raised her voice and disconnected the call. She looked agitated.

"Why are you so upset?" Asked Mr. Tripathi.

"Upset? Your son has gone mad. For the past three days, he has been advising me—Reach there on time. You won't find a girl like her. She is perfect for me. Meet with her and fix the marriage date. He is instructing me on what to do and what not to do."

"Good! At least someone is there in this house to instruct you." Mr. Tripathi and Sanjay exchanged a sheepish smile and nod.

"He is just excited, and he doesn't know how to express it. The new journey is about to begin; you should be happy for him rather than angry over such petty things."

Mrs. Tripathi clearly looked unconvinced by her husband's response and walked inside with heavy footsteps.

"She can hold a grudge for a lifetime, Sanjay. Long back, I once exchanged a watch she had gifted me, not because I didn't like it, but for some reason, ever since then, she returns anything I gift her." Mr. Tripathi whispered with a subtle hint.

At Sharma Sadan, all the arrangements were in place, and Kashvi was asked to get ready as well.

"Show me the saree that you are going to wear today." All of a sudden, Kiran Aunty asked Kashvi.

Kashvi hesitated. She was aware of the usual traits of a woman. Whatever you show them, they will undeniably ask you to change it at the last moment. Mrs. Sharma heard and chipped in on time.

"Let me show you the saree, Kiran," and requested Kashvi to arrange and set aside the jewelry and bangles she had to wear with the saree.

At first, Kashvi was confused, but soon the mother and daughter exchanged glances, and Kashvi had realized her mother's indication.

Kiran Aunty helped her in draping the saree. She looked elegant in her rich tussar silk saree, paired with an embroidered blouse. She adorned her neck with a thin, graceful necklace and paired it with matching studs. She piled a few bangles, pushed them over her knuckles, but then realized Praneel had asked her to wear the bracelet— the same bracelet that she wore when she met him for the first time. She kept the bangles aside and quickly looked for the bracelet, but she couldn't find the bracelet anywhere in her bag.

"Don't delay further. It is a small bracelet; it must be lost," Neelam Aunty remarked, picking up the bangles and helping her put them on. She put a tiny bindi on her forehead. She looked at the bangles and was upset that she couldn't find the bracelet. Her aunt asked her to relax and smile. The feeling of losing that bracelet was unusual for her.

While she was lost in her thoughts, she heard Neelam Aunt saying, "Kashvi, we will call you; you can sit and relax in the room."

By now, Kashvi knew that the potential bride or groom was expected to make a surprise entry in these meetings.

"Oh, these customs make you feel awkward and stupid at the same time." She smiled.

It was almost 3:10 PM when Praneel's family arrived at her uncle's place. His aunts and uncles had also accompanied his parents (Mr. and Mrs. Tripathi). Neelam Aunty was right; it was a ceremony held only in the presence of close family members. Viren Uncle welcomed them all inside his house.

"Did you have any trouble finding this place? Hope my directions helped," Raghu Uncle asked curiously.

"Oh, it was quite helpful with all those landmarks, I must say. You are good at directing people," Mr. Tripathi replied and apologized for being late by a few minutes.

"You must be aware of how much time these ladies take to get ready," Mr. Tripathi mocked.

Raghu Uncle showed them the way to their courtyard. The courtyard was open and spacious, easily accommodating a crowd for a small function. Though there were about 12 people, including Kashvi and her family, her uncle thought it would be the best place for this small function. They all took their seats.

Water and juices were served along with sweets and snacks. Slowly, they all started talking, but Mrs. Tripathi remained quiet and looked curious from the moment she entered the house. Kashvi's aunts and Mrs. Sharma noticed Mrs. Tripathi's sour face and had been trying to talk to her to make her feel comfortable. Finally, Viren Uncle asked Praneel's mom if she was okay. He also added that she looked tired to hide the intention behind his question.

Before she could reply, Mr. Tripathi answered, "Nothing, she is anxious to meet her daughter-in-law."

Everybody laughed, and Mrs. Tripathi stared at Mr. Tripathi, certainly with an expression of not liking his joke.

"We are anxious too, but we don't have a choice, and we have to wait till Praneel returns to India," Kiran Aunty commented, stating her point.

"Can you please call Kashvi? We want to meet her first," Mrs. Tripathi said with a grim face. Everybody was a bit astonished by her response, but her aunt ignored her and went inside to call Kashvi.

Kashvi followed Kiran Aunty and then quietly sat next to her mother. Mrs. Tripathi kept staring at her. Some time had passed, and Mrs. Tripathi slowly stood up and sat next to Kashvi. The gab and the laughter were wrapped in eerie silence. Despite the smiles, the energy felt low in the courtyard. Mrs. Tripathi took Kashvi's hand. Kashvi's eyelids fluttered, and a faint and hesitant smile touched her lips.

"The skin tone of her hands doesn't match that of her face and neck." Mrs. Tripathi snapped at Kashvi.

Before the smile could have spread on Kashvi's face, Mrs. Tripathi's sharp words stole the smile from her face.

Unexpectedly, there was a silence in the room, and Kashvi noticed everybody's reactions had changed. Kashvi could sense the uneasiness in the room, but she could not ask or even stare at the people sitting in the courtyard to find out what had caused this upheaval.

Mrs. Tripathi rose from her place and left the courtyard; "At least talk to her once." Mr. Tripathi followed her, murmuring at her shoulder.

"My son is fair-skinned and handsome. This cannot be a marriage match," with a dissatisfied expression, she ended her sentence, declaring to Mr. Tripathi.

There was some exchange of views and dialogue among themselves, but they did not come inside. His uncle (Sanjay) was moving from one corner to the other, holding his phone to his right ear.

His parents were still out, discussing something continuously. After a few minutes, Viren and Raghu Uncle stood up and went outside to find out what the matter was. She looked outside again and saw Raghu Uncle's expression changing; he was losing his patience after listening to their explanation. Viren Uncle looked stressed.

Soon, she saw her aunts and mother going out to join the harangue. Kashvi moved her eyeballs around, looking from one end to another of the courtyard, as there was hardly anyone with her. The conversation between the families didn't appear as a two-way discussion, and Praneel's family looked uninterested. She saw Praneel's mom making a call and talking to someone.

Mrs. Tripathi stayed on the call; Mrs. Sharma and her aunts (Neelam and Kiran) came inside with unreceptive faces. Neelam Aunty was talking under her breath with Mrs. Sharma, "Let her talk to the guy; they cannot give such lame reasons now."

Kashvi knew something was wrong, but couldn't dare to ask anyone. Her heart was pounding, and she felt flustered and nervous. Within 20-30 minutes, Kashvi saw everyone leaving the house. Her uncles did not show any cordiality, and their faces looked stern.

Kashvi still did not understand what exactly had happened. She could make out that there was a discordance between her and Praneel's family. Her mother was distressed by this incident and was sitting in the corner of the room.

Raghu and Viren Uncle came in and asked Kashvi to go inside the room. She couldn't gather the courage to ask anything as they all looked furious. Her feet were numb, and she struggled to walk. When she was about to enter her room, she heard her uncle saying, 'Just because their son is fair-skinned, they cannot comment about our daughter's skin color. She is not an object. They cannot come, see, and reject her, looking at her complexion.'

Kashvi was staggered by his words, and her intuition was correct. They rejected her because they felt she was not fair-skinned, and this could not be a perfect match for their son. Kashvi changed her dress and washed her face; she looked into the mirror. She looked at her face, her neck, and her hands. She could decipher the reason behind that silence now when she had entered the courtyard. She could read everyone's expression and the disapproval in their stare when she followed her aunt. They disliked her because of her dusky skin tone. She didn't meet their expectations —the standard of ideal beauty: a fair-skinned girl.

The unpardonable offense of having a darker complexion than Praneel. She felt humiliated and perplexed that people could dislike someone just because of their skin color. If looks are so important, how do character, behavior, and etiquette matter?

"You can be dishonest and rude, but you cannot lack the desired skin tone," she explained to herself, trying to see clearly in the mirror.

She slowly wiped her face, fighting with her thoughts. She took the bangles and kept them inside the jewelry box. She noticed a tiny object shining under a necklace placed in one of the sections of the box. She held the string to pull the object outside and realized it was her bracelet and Praneel's lucky charm. She kept it back in the box with a disheartened feeling and closed the lid.

She sat quietly inside her room and didn't know how to react at that moment. She gathered courage and went outside, where everybody was sitting. Everybody looked at Kashvi.

"The guy likes you and wants to marry you, but his parents are confused. You don't have to stress yourself. It is their problem now. Let them decide what they want," Viren Uncle replied with a stern expression.

Things change at a fast pace. He was referred to as a 'guy' until their first meeting, then called by his name, 'Praneel,' when he agreed to their proposal.

He is referred to as a 'guy' again after his parents' meeting.

X
The Disagreement

The lively house had turned dull. Neelam Aunty had rearranged the house, especially the courtyard. Her uncles were sharing their views with her mother, and her mother seemed confused by all the different suggestions coming in from her relatives about Praneel's family. Her aunt served dinner and called everyone to the table. She suggested not discussing this topic further and letting everyone have dinner in peace. Kashvi did not feel like eating, but she ate because she did not want her mother to see that Kashvi was pining for something.

She was always fearless and was never dependent on anyone. But this was not the case today; her heart was still beating fast, and she was deeply hurt not just by Praneel's parents' behavior, but by everyone who ever came to defend her skin color.

According to Kashvi, this is not a topic for debate or why they have to defend someone's appearance.

'Is it really so bad or harmful that they have to justify it in front of his parents? How does it really matter? Why did they feel the need to explain her worth when compared with their fair-skinned son? Why does society always need acceptance from everyone?' She had forgotten that it is a patriarchal society, where men and their families still have a controlling position, and it will take hundreds of years to change this mindset.

She controlled her anger and decided to go for a walk to calm herself. She didn't want to talk to anyone, not even her mother. As Kashvi stepped out, Mr. Sharma called her from behind, "Where are you going? It is too late."

Kashvi didn't want to answer, but she couldn't do that with her; she knew her mother was worried.

"Going for a walk to breathe some fresh air. It is suffocating inside." She did not make any eye contact with her mother. She opened the door with heavy footsteps and went out without closing it. After taking two rounds of the park, she was infuriated. With every step, the sadness evaporated, and anger was fuming inside her.

She took her mobile out and called Praneel. Things have changed drastically in a few hours. This was one of the few times when Kashvi had called him. In the last few months, the only complaint Praneel had from Kashvi was that she never calls him. He looked at the mobile and saw her name flashing on the screen. When he was ever ready to pick up her call, the one call which could have overwhelmed him had made him nervous today; his heart was beating fast. He picked up the call, and Kashvi asked if he could talk for a few minutes.

"Yes," he said in a hoarse voice.

She paused and controlled her anger.

"They didn't come to meet me, Praneel. They were here to see whether I would be the best fit for their son."

The other side of the line was silent for the first time.

"How would you feel if someone met you and stared at you as if you were some objects that had been put up on display? Imagine people looking at you to decide whether the shade of this person would be suitable for display when they place it in their house." She said sharply.

"Tell me, how would you feel? You have asked me enough questions and probed me for explanations over the past few months. It is your time to answer me now."

Praneel was speechless. He wanted to console her, but he sensed the anger and pain in her voice and couldn't muster the courage to speak a single word. There was a queue of questions from someone who had just patiently listened to anything and everything he would have said or blabbered on the call.

Her voice was stern, unlike the calm she always sounded. This was a different side of Kashvi, which Praneel was aware of but had never faced.

"They were not there to meet me; they came to choose me," Kashvi's voice trembled with anger and pain.

"I know whatever had happened was not right. I know how you would have felt. I don't have answers to any of your questions right now. Give me some time. I am talking to them." Praneel replied.

Kashvi disconnected the call. She had got the answer; she had an intuitive sense and could understand people with a single reply. This was something Kashvi was mentally prepared for, and that is why she was reluctant to talk to Praneel initially. She had also brought up the topic with Praneel to gauge his reaction and support. Praneel had clearly expressed his views and love for Kashvi, but actions speak louder than words. You can have your views and opinions about anything, but when it comes to taking action, very few people can do what is right. Only a handful of people dare to question the conservative mindset, particularly when these thoughts are rooted in a family.

She had also discussed her concerns with her friend, Sarika. Upon her confirmation and justification, she decided to turn her back on this topic, considering her habit of over-analyzing things and fretting too much might ruin things between her and Praneel.

Most of the time, your intuitions are correct. It is just that you fail to accept it at the right time. The more you delay or ignore the problem, the more you suffer in the end.

Though Kashvi's upbringing was conventional and in a small town, her mother had instilled empathy in her. She instilled ethics and social responsibility in her and always encouraged her to take the proper steps when she saw anything wrong. She might talk less when she is in front of a crowd or hesitate to reply, not because she is afraid of someone, but because she never wanted to hurt anyone. She always believed that a person's mouth—home to the strongest muscle in the body—could do immense damage. A single wrong word spoken in anger could hit harder than a physical attack and irreparably hurt someone. When it came to taking the right action, she had always done so, whether in her school days or in the office. In her childhood, when some girls were reluctant to play with a disabled kid in their society, she was the one who came forward and became her friend. For the first few days, nobody played with them, but then slowly they all started playing together, seeing and learning from Kashvi's inclusive behavior. In her office, she spoke up for the housekeeping staff when they had to use a separate space outside the office building for drinking water. Kashvi felt it was wrong and initiated having a common space for drinking water. The only thing people should be worried about is cleanliness and hygiene, not the designation, which determines where they can have food or water, just because they are at different levels in the organization.

This was the time when she had to take a step for herself. She had decided on the next right step for her life, but when you are in love, you always wait and give a second chance. It is easy to question the world, but it is difficult to question your loved ones.

Kashvi arrived back. She opened the door and found everyone sitting in the hall, waiting for her. Though they all looked at Kashvi's face in the hope of some positive reply, their stares gave her a shiver as these glares reminded her of the incident that had happened in the evening. She tried to avoid everyone and started climbing the stairs to the room.

Her mother asked, "What happened? Have you tried reaching him?"

Kashvi stopped at the stairs, holding the support. She turned and replied, "Yes, anything wrong in that?"

"What is he saying?" Mrs. Sharma questioned.

"What should he say? They are his parents. You cannot expect someone to rebel against his family for a girl and for something that had happened in his absence."

She wanted to prepare her mother for the worst that could happen tomorrow, and more than her, she was reminding herself by answering back to her mother.

Before her mother could inquire further, she added that "Praneel needs some time, and he is talking to his parents." She wanted to think of something positive, but the only thing that was on her mind was the meeting with Praneel's family. Everything was flashing in front of her eyes, which she did not want to think of. She came back to bed to sleep and looked at the screen. There was no call or message from Praneel. She was disheartened looking at the phone, which had been a burden for her until yesterday. This reminded her of Sarika's statement when she heard Kashvi saying that she would be relaxed if Praneel did not call her: "I will ask the same question when you are *deeply in love with him. I bet you will regret your response that you just blurted out in front of me.*"

Sarika was right; Kashvi regretted her response. She kept her phone out of reach and lay down. She closed her eyes tightly to fall asleep. She could hear her mother and uncle talking about Praneel's family. Everyone offered many suggestions about what they could have done to calm the situation or how Praneel's presence would have prevented it.

Neelam Aunty also mentioned that maybe they just came to say no, and that is why they did not want him to be part of today's function. There were so many speculations going around the house, making it even more difficult for Kashvi to fall asleep.

Kashvi wanted to tell everyone to stop mulling over these things, but she couldn't. She wanted to call Praneel and complain about everything, but she couldn't. She wanted to tell her mother to do something and make everything normal again, like it used to be, but she couldn't. She wanted to call Praneel to check whether he could fix everything, but she couldn't. She recalled the words that Praneel spoke to her when she was stressed one day. It was playing in the back of her mind.

"There is a solution to every problem. It is up to us whether we want to accept it or not. If you don't have a solution, then accept the problem and live with it."

XI
The Arranged Breakup

Soon after meeting Kashvi, Praneel's mother called to inform him about the decision she had made. Praneel had envisioned his future with Kashvi. A life with a partner with whom he felt loved, trusted, and respected. Praneel was not prepared for this situation and was shaken to hear the peculiar remark she made about Kashvi, who holds a special place in his heart.

Mrs. Tripathi questioned his decision, and their discussion soon turned into an argument. Since then, Praneel had been on continuous calls with his parents. He was trying to convince his parents, but was unable to understand why they did not like Kashvi. According to him, she was perfect. He tried to explain everything he liked about her, but it was all in vain. His parents were angry and couldn't believe their son could go against them, that too for a girl whom he had just met through a marriage proposal. Praneel was in shock and had not imagined that such a situation would arise.

The same night, after talking to Kashvi, he called his mother again.

He patiently asked what was happening at their end. Mrs. Tripathi was still furious and replied in an angry tone, "How could it be? You have given so much stress to your father and me. You have gone blind and mad after meeting that girl. You don't even care about us anymore. I have given birth to you, and your father has done so much for you that you will never be able to pay us back, even if you try to count and return in money. You are so selfish, and you are only thinking about yourself. What does a parent want from their son? A good daughter-in-law who ..." Before she could complete her last statement, Praneel cut her off.

"What is the definition of a good daughter-in-law for you?"

Mrs. Tripathi did not have an answer to his question, but she did not want to put her foot down in front of him. When parents cannot justify or win a battle against their children, they roll the dice and play emotionally.

For three continuous hours, he was on call and answered every single doubt that his parents had. He understood they would never agree and accept Kashvi. He was furious and could no longer control his anger.

"I love her and want to marry her, and I really do not understand why you are doing this to me. If this were the case, why have you both agreed and asked me to go and meet her? Why did you not mention that you don't need someone who I love, you need a daughter-in-law of your choice? You need a showpiece."

Mrs. Tripathi remained silent.

"Oh, how can I forget you want me to marry your friend's daughter, right? That is never going to happen."

Mrs. Tripathi did not answer, and he disconnected the call.

He flung his hand with the intent of throwing his phone, but controlled himself as it was the only means he could use at that point in time to resolve the situation, and tossed it angrily on his bed.

He sat on the chair in the corner of his room, placing his palms over his face. He kept clenching his fists in anger.

He wanted to call Kashvi, but he couldn't. He wanted to tell her everything he was trying to do to make things better from his end, but he couldn't. He wanted to tell her how much he loves her, but he couldn't. He was emotionally drained and at last sat down facing toward the balcony and could only see dark clouds. The sky was not clear. There were no stars, and it looked like it might rain at any time. Dawn was about to break, and Praneel had dozed off on the chair.

When he woke up, his neck was hurting, but this pain was less than the pain he had experienced in his life so far. He was exhausted and had a nasty headache.

The feeling of dejection had settled somewhere deep in his heart. Looking outside, he saw no sign of sunlight; it was a gloomy day. He went to his bed and picked up his phone. He noticed there were a few missed calls from his client. He was not in the mood to go to work, so he called his manager and informed him that he would be on leave today.

"Hope you are doing well. This client is a little difficult and makes a fuss of everything. Let me know if you need anything there," his manager asked with a concerned voice.

"Yes, it is a sinus headache because of which I could not sleep and want to take rest," he replied.

"Take care; close this project, and return as soon as possible," his boss replied.

He hung up the phone and looked at the messages. There was no message or call from Kashvi. By noon, his phone rang, and it was his father's call. He picked up the call.

"What have you decided?" Mr. Tripathi asked.

"How does this really matter?" he wanted to reply, but he stopped himself from speaking. After a deliberate pause, he asked, "For what?"

When are you going to call the girl and say you cannot marry her? His father asked hastily and sternly.

Why would I do that? Praneel replied.

I have already told Mom that I want to marry her. It is you and Mom who are not ready for some stupid reason.

I have not called you to listen to your speech, Mr. Tripathi replied. "You have to call and inform them."

I am never going to do that, Praneel answered his father.

Your mother is not well, Praneel. We do not want any drama now. Let us close this.

'Drama?' Praneel was speechless and angry. 'What has happened to Mom?' She was fine until yesterday.

You have troubled her so much; she is in grief and has not eaten anything since yesterday. She never expected that you would fight with her and disrespect her, his father replied.

Disrespect? Why can't you both understand what I am going through right now? I need your support, he pleaded, trying to control his anger. 'Please don't do this to me.'

"Forget her or forget us," Mr. Tripathi disconnected the call.

Rejection and failures are also crucial parts of life. If you face problems and failures with small milestones, you are always prepared to face bigger challenges. You know how to resolve them.

For Praneel, life was always easy-going and straightforward. He was from a well-established family and had never faced struggle or rejection in any phase of his life. He had consistently received and earned things in his life without any difficulty. His parents had never denied anything that Praneel had asked or demanded from them.

For marriage, he had never thought that it wouldn't be his choice. He had made it clear to his parents that he would meet the girl they had proposed, but in the end, it should be his choice. He couldn't believe that he couldn't make the most critical decision of his life.

This was the first time he had faced rejection. After long debates, arguments, and fights, he couldn't convince his parents. His day went on with calls, fighting, and pleading with his parents. He had no idea what his next step should be.

The whole day, Kashvi waited for Praneel's call, but her phone did not ring. Although after yesterday's incident, nobody in the house wanted their daughter to be part of Praneel's family, people still try to see a ray of hope even in the worst situations. They try to find something good even in someone who has hurt them.

Raghu Uncle called Mr. Tripathi to find out what had been decided. Somewhere, everybody in the family was aware of their decision, but everything needs to end formally.

Mr. Tripathi picked up the call and answered.

"No, we cannot approve this relation; you can consider 'no' from our side." He replied in a cold voice.

Raghu Uncle made a final attempt.

"But you mentioned you needed your son's consent. If he agrees, you won't have any issues in this relationship."

His father had no response to this question, so he covered up. "No, I believe he will not go against our wishes. You can convey the same to Mrs. Sharma. Moreover, my son is naive and gullible. Whenever someone shares their problems with him, he gets carried away. We believe the same would have happened in Gwalior when he would have met Mrs. Sharma. She would have shared her struggles in raising Kashvi after Mr. Sharma's death, and he would have felt sorry for her. As a result, he would not have been able to say 'no'.

Raghu Uncle ended the call and recounted everything to Mrs. Sharma. Kashvi was listening to everything sitting inside the room. Her uncle called Kashvi and asked for her opinion.

"Do you still want to marry Praneel? You have already seen his parents' attitude; there is no match between our families. We definitely don't want our daughter to get married into this family. You will never be happy there," her uncle clarified his reasoning.

"What do you want to do? You have to decide now." Mrs. Sharma pressed Kashvi for the answer.

Kashvi quietly listened to everything and dialed Praneel.

Praneel picked up the call.

"You wanted to marry me out of pity," her voice was shaking in anger.

"What nonsense are you talking about?"

"Uncle just mentioned on the call."

"And you believed it? It has been nearly a year now, more than 314 days. You would not even know exactly how many days, Kashvi, and yet you trust whatever these elders are saying." He answered with pain in his voice.

He searched for better words to explain and clear up the misunderstandings. She stopped him.

"What have you decided?" she asked.

"I really don't know anything at this point. I am trying to make them understand."

"If you don't know, then you accept the problem and live with it," Kashvi replied and disconnected the call.

Kashvi came into the room where her uncle and mother were sitting.

Her uncle looked at Kashvi, "They will never give consent to this relationship even if Praneel tries his best, and we feel, Kashvi, that they don't deserve you."

Her hands were still trembling with anger, so she dialed Mr. Tripathi.

Hello Uncle!

Hello!

'I heard that your son accepted this proposal out of sympathy.'

'Ahh, you know, Praneel is soft-headed.' Mr. Tripathi spoke in a meek voice.

'And in his innocence, he used to call me four times a day?' She retorted.

'What I meant was,' he tried correcting his statement.

'What an 'unpretentious' gesture, Uncle? It is good that you rejected this proposal. I am certainly uncomfortable being part of such a modest family.'

'Kashvi, what I meant was,' before Mr. Tripathi could complete his sentence, she disconnected the call.

Broken and shattered, she sat in the courtyard.

Children are often blamed for lying, nagging, and complaining, but elders are masters at making false stories to achieve their objectives. Kids do it in ignorance, and adults do it knowingly. The irony is, if you question them, you are labeled as a 'culprit'.

Kashvi accepted the decision with a heavy heart, thinking they had **arranged it** and **broken it up**.

XII
The Return

Daytime drags on, but the nights are awfully depressing when you break up. That night was apparently interminable with the outlandish situation. They were pondering the clashes and differences they had never had between them. Both of them were mulling over the circumstances that had changed their lives in the blink of an eye.

What could have been done differently to avoid this situation? Was this destined to happen? Had my presence avoided this situation?

Was I too naive? Wasn't I forced to be in this situation? Had I not gone with the flow? Was it the wrong time and the right person? Or was it the right time and the wrong person? Things would have been different if I had listened to my intuition.

Praneel and Kashvi grappled with unanswered questions and unresolved issues within themselves.

The train tickets were for Saturday night, but Mrs. Sharma wanted to return home before Saturday. Mrs.

Sharma was behind Kashvi to reschedule the tickets. She did not want to stay there anymore. She felt that they had come to that city for some good reason and that somehow things did not work out, so what was the point of staying there for another day?

The place and people around us make a big difference. Kashvi knew she had family here, and with them, it was easier to forget her pain. She explained to her mom and uncle that it was not the end of the world.

Saturday morning, Kashvi packed her bag. While putting her things in the bag, she started recalling every conversation she had over the phone with Praneel—the constant assurance, 'Nothing will go wrong because I am with you.'

She remembered how carefully her mother had folded and kept the saree inside the bag, which Kashvi had to wear for the meeting—'the special saree for the very special occasion for my daughter'.

She recollected the happy and calm expression of her mother, which she had seen after a long time since her father passed away.

She remembered her uncle's satisfied face—'keeping his promise he had made to his elder brother'.

In the corner of her mind, she started blaming herself. "Everything was going fine until I came into the picture. It all collapsed because of me, my skin color."

After packing her bag, she left the room and sat with her cousins, who had come to meet her. She was engaging herself by spending time with her family members. She was trying hard to hide her feelings, but the somber mood had taken root deep in her heart.

In the evening, to divert her mind, she went into the kitchen to help her aunt pack the food for the train journey. Kashvi wrapped the puris and placed them inside the box with some pickles.

"It is a late-night train; we will reach early in the morning, so there is no need to pack food," she told her aunt.

"It is always good to pack something for travel; you never know when you need it," her aunt replied.

"Shall I keep some sweets with it?"

Kashvi immediately declined and turned her face away. A lot of sweet boxes were stacked next to the refrigerator. These were the same boxes that her uncle had packed to gift to Praneel's family.

"I never knew that, along with humans, even a non-living thing could cause so much pain." She whispered, ignoring those sweet boxes.

If you like someone, you tend to disregard the bigger issues to keep the connection alive. If you dislike someone, you will find numerous flaws to drift apart. This is a typical way of thinking for a human being. Is being fair-skinned really so crucial in our society, and being dark an unacceptable problem? **You can be a troublemaker, but you cannot be dark in this country.**

"Aunty, throw those sweets away as they would not be good for anyone to consume." She suggested placing the water bottle under the tap of a water filter. The bitterness was clearly audible in her words.

She stepped outside the kitchen, wrapping the food box in a plastic bag and tying its strings to keep it from spilling. Mrs. Sharma was sitting in the living room, ready to leave. Watching everything from the sidelines, she felt helpless for the first time. "Why was I unable to do anything for my daughter?" Guilt preyed on her mind as she held herself responsible; she was as culpable as everyone in that courtyard.

"Have you booked an autorickshaw?" Mrs. Sharma asked her brother-in-law.

"I will drop you. Why do you want to go by autorickshaw?" Her uncle took the car out of the garage, which was adjacent to their lawn.

"Do not worry, everything will be fine. It must be God's blessing that we came to know the real faces of these people in time. Kashvi, too, will be fine soon." Her aunt was reassuring her mother.

Kashvi had gone upstairs to ensure she had not left anything in the room. As she left the room, the flare of the oil lamp in the prayer space drew her attention. She knelt to seek God's blessing. She knew it was easy with family members, but going back to her home would remind her of everything about Praneel, which would be a tough time for her.

With her hands folded in prayer, she prayed to God for the courage to deal with this heartbreak.

Kashvi climbed down and greeted her aunt to take her leave. Her aunt hugged her.

"You are my brave child. Forget that guy; you deserve better," her aunt said. Though Kashvi knew her aunt's intentions were good, she did not like a single word of what she had just spoken and gave a faint smile in response.

Looking at the city's lane on the way to the railway station reminded her of her arrival in this city. A few days back, there was so much excitement and happiness in her life that had suddenly vanished. It was filled with pain and sorrow. She, too, wanted to leave this city as soon as possible. They soon reached the station and walked fast with their luggage to reach the platform.

The train was on time, and they found a bench to sit on. Kashvi was trying not to face her mom. Every time Kashvi looked at her, she saw disappointment, which was even more painful. Raghu Uncle went to a tea stall and bought two cups of tea in earthen cups. He knew that Kashvi loves having tea in the earthen cup, but today even that tea and the aroma of that earthen cup couldn't help her relieve her agony. She felt a hollowness inside her heart; she was in shock and perplexed—what's next? What kind of unpleasant feeling is this? She was unable to express or tell anyone about it.

Her uncle was talking to her mother and was telling her not to worry about Kashvi. She will be fine soon, but also advised her mother to act normally and pretend to be happy. According to him, seeing her mother disheartened might also adversely affect Kashvi.

"If you are worried about that day's incident, just forget it. All these things happen, and hardly any marriage is fixed in the first attempt."

Her uncle also mentioned that he has some other proposals and will talk to their parents. Kashvi knowingly ignored her uncle's recommendation.

People are often casual when questioning or confronting old beliefs and norms. Instead of objecting, they accept these practices, making them part of daily life, the primary reason certain regressive customs persist in our society. **The race of finding a groom resumed, and nobody cared that Kashvi was going through a tough time.**

Every time someone said, "Forget about that guy," her heart sank a little deeper, flooded with memories. She was disconcerted by their suggestions and wondered how easy it was for everyone to say this. It reminded her of the first day. Everyone praised 'the guy' as perfect, and his family was one of the most respected families in their society. This was the best proposal that her uncle had scrutinized from his long list. They all persuaded Kashvi to accept it without giving it a single thought.

The situation has changed. She observed people talking just the opposite, and among all of them, the bitter one was, 'Forget that guy.'

Upon that, they also suggested that there are several other proposals, somewhere hinting that she should prepare herself to marry another guy.

While Kashvi was battling with her agony, the whistle of the train distracted her. She promptly caught hold of her bags. Her uncle was talking loudly with her mom, which she or anybody could hardly hear with the tumult of the train's arrival and passengers' rush on the platform. She scooted off quickly toward the coach, looked back, and called her mother. Her mother was walking as fast as she could, and Raghu Uncle was helping her with her bag. He helped them keep their luggage safe and bid them adieu.

The train left the platform. Kashvi was looking outside the window. She was exhausted, but not sleepy. Most of the passengers had already slept. Mrs. Sharma looked at her daughter and asked her to sleep. Kashvi did not speak, but lay down and covered herself with the blanket. The train was chugging fast, and so was Kashvi's heart. She closed her eyes and wondered if it was all a dream.

What if everything had settled down by the time she reached home? She knew that whatever she thought was a dream and would never become reality.

Human minds run in several directions before they accept reality. They dream and prefer false stories.

The next morning, the train reached the destination. After a bumpy auto ride, they reached their home. Mrs. Sharma unlocked the gate while Kashvi took the bags out of the auto. She paid the auto driver and made her way inside the house.

"Looks like there was a storm; there is so much dust everywhere in the house. It will take time to clean and organize things back, especially these window glasses, and look at these plants," her mother said, pointing to the indoor climbers that had turned dry and pale.

"We need to water them."

Kashvi slowly climbed the stairs, dragging the bags, and dropped them into the room. She felt that some burden was released. Without wasting much time, she began cleaning the house.

"Let's freshen up and have some tea, then we can clean the house, Kashvi."

"I hate this mess and can't stand it even for a minute. I want everything back the way it was before I left for Indore."

Her mom understood Kashvi's intentions, but she avoided showing any resistance to her reaction. It took an hour to clean the house. After taking a shower, she plunked down on a chair kept in the living area. Mrs. Sharma had already prepared tea and poha.

"Let some sun rays come inside; the house was closed for so many days," and instructed Kashvi to open the terrace door.

Her silence bothered her mother, particularly when she ate without commenting on the breakfast. Mrs. Sharma knew that her daughter would not complain about anything that happened to her in Indore. She wouldn't even talk and would never bring up Praneel's topic.

Everybody is different. Some people argue with their dear ones, some cry, and some never talk about their problems when they are deeply hurt. Kashvi was the latter. Her mom never liked this attitude of hers. Mrs. Sharma always wanted her daughter to speak up and discuss things, but she never did.

Kashvi had read the same page several times. This was the first time she couldn't understand what she was reading. She jumped again and again to the first paragraph of the page, but she could not finish it even after a few hours. She flipped the book and placed it upside down on the bed. Mrs. Sharma's worry continued to rise. Her daughter had not uttered a single word since breakfast. The sole way she could think of was to call her friend, Sarika. She had already informed Sarika about their meeting with Praneel's family.

As the sunlight faded, the birds began returning to their nests. The quiet evening was filled with the chirping of these birds, and Sarika opened the main gate, calling her friend's name and greeting Mrs. Sharma as she climbed up the stairs.

"Where is Kashvi?" she asked.

"Terrace." Mrs. Sharma answered in a low tone. Sarika was about to climb up, but Mrs. Sharma called her again. "Sarika, I know whatever has happened was not right, but try talking to her and find out what is going on in her mind. We both know she won't speak up and share anything with anyone."

"Don't worry, aunty, she will be fine."

"You are her best friend. Try your best to help her get out of all these things."

"Everything takes time," Sarika assured her, holding her hand. She walked up to meet her dear friend.

Kashvi was standing on the edge, holding the boundary support. She was staring at the road.

"Are you thinking of jumping off the terrace?" Sarika mocked.

"Why would I do that?" Kashvi replied and looked at her from the corner of her eye.

Sarika smiled.

They both stood there for an hour, watching the roads fill with traffic and slowly grow abandoned. Sarika was quiet for a long time, which was a difficult task for her.

Finally, she broke the silence.

"I came here to meet you, Kashvi, and you are not even talking to me. What are you thinking?"

"Nothing," Kashvi replied.

"Has he called you since then?"

"No," answered Kashvi in a shaking voice.

"How can he do that?" Sarika uttered.

"Have you tried calling him?" Sarika asked.

"No," replied Kashvi.

"Tell me what he exactly mentioned after all this," Sarika inquired.

"He said he tried convincing his parents in every different way, and he doesn't know what to do."

"Have you said anything to him?" she asked again.

"What do you mean by anything? Should I have pleaded in front of him, 'Please leave your parents aside and marry me?' Is that what you mean by anything?" Kashvi asked her back.

"No," replied Sarika immediately, and then slowly muttered, "or maybe something along similar lines, you could have said."

Kashvi gave her a glaring look, and she turned her face away from her.

"Do you know something?" They turned to one another.

"Either he will come back, and you will agree to spend the rest of your life with him, or he will not. Whatever will happen will happen at its own pace, and it will take a lot of time. You cannot stay like this forever."

"What is meant by 'like this forever'?"

"You know very well what I am trying to say. You need to talk to your mom and me. Open up and say whatever you feel; otherwise, it will hurt you and might harm you mentally in the long run."

"I know, Mom would have told you all this. If I am not talking, that doesn't mean I am upset. I am absolutely fine."

"Alright. Let us go down; the sun has set, and it is dark now. I cannot stand with you here and get bitten by mosquitoes. You might not be feeling it because you are going through a different pain now, but I am," Sarika blabbered.

"Don't make fun of it," Kashvi replied in anger as they climbed down the stairs.

After dinner, Sarika left for her home. The time Kashvi had been trying to escape had struck. You cannot always surround yourself with people and engage yourself in work to run away from the sombre feeling you carry in your heart. You need to deal with your problem alone.

The clock had struck nine, and with the minute hand moving closer to four, her heart kept beating faster. Every single word of Praneel was buzzing in her ears; she wanted to forget everything, but it was not so easy. She switched her phone off and turned her face to the wall.

The paint on the wall appeared dull and gloomy. With her constant glare, she could notice the rough texture, minor cracks, some spots, and patches on the wall. In the silence of the night, her endless complaints were swallowed by the wall.

"I will soon paint this wall with a different shade, and the room will be lively again."

Her alarm clock rang, and she realized she had been awake all night. She did not feel like going to the office. Her heart was beating fast, and she had a throbbing headache. She stood up and felt dizzy. She knew something was not going well with her. She took a bath and got ready for the office.

"What would you like to have for breakfast?" Mrs. Sharma asked, watching the news.

"Nothing, just give me a cup of tea."

She sat in the room, staring at the television, feeling that uneasiness had seized her. The mobile was lying next to her; she pulled it closer and dropped a message to her manager that she wouldn't come to the office today. She ploddingly walked into her room and dropped herself onto the bed. Her mother followed her and asked if she was okay.

"I have a bad headache, and I'm not feeling good," she said, turning her face again to the wall and closing her eyes. Her mother sat beside her and applied a pain-relieving oil to her forehead.

"You need to talk. Please share with me, Kashvi. I am your mother, and I understand your pain."

Kashvi did not move; her mother noticed she had fallen asleep. Her mother got up cautiously and came into the hall. Kashvi's phone was ringing. It was Sarika's call. "What happened, aunty? Kashvi had not come to the office today. Is everything fine?" Sarika was worried about her friend. Her mother informed her about Kashvi's health in a hushed tone.

"Ok, don't worry, you take care of her. I will come and meet her in the evening," Sarika answered from the other side of the call.

Three hours had passed. Kashvi woke up but did not talk much. She kept walking from room to living area, from dining space to terrace, terrace to ground floor. Her mother noticed Kashvi was trying to engage herself in regular chores, but couldn't focus on anything for a long time.

In the evening, she took a cup of tea and sat on the stairs that led to the open terrace from the living room.

Sarika had also returned from the office and was talking to her mother inside the kitchen.

"I need a cup of tea," she said, and then went and sat next to her friend.

"What happened? Why did you not come to the office today?"

"I am not feeling well," her voice trembled. Sarika had never heard her friend sound like this.

"How do you feel?" Sarika gathered courage and asked.

"I don't know. I have palpitations. I cannot sleep. I feel blank. I don't want to listen to or even see anyone right now. I am neither sad nor angry. I don't have words to express how I feel."

Sarika knew her friend was sad and broken. She needed help to overcome all this. She couldn't see her friend in such a condition, who was always brave and strong.

"No problem, let us go inside," Sarika replied.

"I cannot," replied Kashvi.

"Why?" Asked Sarika.

"I feel like my legs are numb. I don't have the strength to walk." Sarika went into the kitchen and brought a glass of water for her friend.

"Have it." Kashvi drank the water and placed the glass by her side.

"How are you feeling now?" asked Sarika.

There was no response from Kashvi, and she kept quiet.

"It is not easy to forget someone so quickly, Kashvi. It will take time. I told you yesterday."

"It is not about forgetting someone." She broke her silence.

"I know how you are feeling, Kashvi."

"No, you don't know how I feel. I feel ashamed. I feel rejected. I feel excluded. Imagine sitting in front of people, all staring at you to evaluate your physical appearance. Their cold expression, the contemptuous stare of his relatives, and the disapproving glance of his mother—I couldn't qualify the beauty parameters they had set for their prospective daughter-in-law. It was a demeaning experience. No one can understand until they experience it. One loses one's sense of worth, Sarika." Her voice trembled and choked.

Sarika knew her sympathetic words would not heal her friend's pain. It was not a momentary sadness of a breakup. It was the damage a meeting had done to her friend, shattering her confidence and crushing her happiness.

"Someone's frivolous behavior shouldn't affect us. Have you ever felt the same because of Praneel?" Sarika mentioned it intentionally to divert her attention from that incident.

"And I should consider it as a consolation prize." Kashvi satirized in a painful voice. "I had always thought that I would marry a guy whom I love. I am not like you, Sarika. Every few months, you date some new guy."

Sarika smiled and said, "You are right. But the last one I dated for a year. Do you remember a few months back, when you asked me in the office parking space why I was not introducing my boyfriend to my parents? This time, I did not break up. He broke up when he heard that I wanted him to meet my family and then marry him. He straight away denied my proposal. I might not have hurt as deeply as you have, but I surely know a bit of your pain and agony."

Her mother was listening to everything, standing behind them.

"I hate this. I hate people cheating each other, making promises, breaking them, and marrying someone else. How can they do that? How can you love one person and marry another person? I cannot do that, and it is not my fault. I was dragged into this relationship forcefully by mom, by uncle, by you, and by Praneel. You know, I was never ready to talk or call him. It was because of all of you that I answered his call. I had always set some boundaries between him and me because I know myself. How and when did I become attached and close to him? How can I do this? I cannot think of anyone taking his place in my life. How can you all say or even think that I should forget him? I will not, and why should I? You all have put me in this situation. I never wanted to be here. Who will help me now? I want to feel normal and happy like I was before. I want to erase him from my memory." Kashvi kept complaining in tears.

Listening to her complaints, her mother was shocked. She realized she had pushed her daughter into this pit, and she didn't know how to pull her out. She slowly moved from there.

Sarika was standing quietly, listening to her friend. She never imagined seeing her dear friend in this situation. Her friend, who was always stern, knew what she wanted in life and had helped others. Sarika held herself accountable because she had only forced Kashvi and brought her close to Praneel.

"Let us go inside, Kashvi. It has been an hour. This won't solve any problem. You know better than I do."

Kashvi picked up her glass and went inside the room. Sarika followed her and saw Mrs. Sharma was cooking in the kitchen. She felt guilty about what she had done to her daughter, honouring the tradition, without knowing the intention behind this meeting. Mrs. Sharma spoke with Sarika and asked whether she should call Praneel. "It is awful to see my daughter like this," she said, blaming herself for it.

"No need to call anyone aunty. I know Kashvi; she will be fine soon," Sarika replied.

"Stay with her tonight. At least, she talks to you." Mrs. Sharma requested Sarika.

Sarika stayed with Kashvi that day. That night, Kashvi talked for hours with Sarika about Praneel, something she had never done in the past few months. It was midnight, and Sarika had fallen asleep. As she lay staring at the ceiling, her phone rang in the hall. She hurried to answer it. It was Praneel's call. She picked up the phone but did not answer.

The line was filled with silence, but something was loud—was it anger or pain?

"Are you there, Kashvi?" Praneel said in a disheartened voice.

Praneel waited to hear Kashvi's voice.

"I know you are angry with me; he paused as he swallowed hard, and you don't want to talk to me."

"At least say something to me?" He wanted to hear her voice, but there was silence on the other end. He did not know whether Kashvi was listening to the call. He waited for a few minutes for Kashvi's response, then disconnected the call with a good-night wish.

He stayed in his room, looking at her name on the screen, cleaning the screen with his right thumb. He realized it was not dust; tears in his eyes had blurred the screen.

After a few days, she resumed her office. Most of her team members were curious to know why her pre-wedding ritual had been called off. People are more interested in other people's lives than in what is happening in their own lives. A snooping team member strolled around Kashvi's desk and was eager to know the reason behind her extended and unplanned leave.

Kashvi kept steering her questions to a different topic. When her colleague's burning curiosity was not satisfied, she left her place with disappointment.

A few hours had passed, and another nosy colleague arrived at her desk and asked about her health. Kashvi knew the reason for her inquisitiveness, so she politely answered with concise responses.

A few more team members had gathered around the other corner of the desk and kept their ears open to acquire some gossip for the day.

"You were supposed to resume yesterday," a colleague asked curiously.

"I had the flu, and the doctor advised me to take precautions and stay away from people for a few more days." She glared at her colleague. After listening to Kashvi's response, they all dispersed.

Sarika moved her chair and asked Kashvi to calm herself. "It is so annoying, Sarika. Why do they poke their noses into others' personal affairs?"

"A few days ago, an overly friendly neighbor who lives just a few houses away visited my home. She, too, wanted to scoop out some information from my mother and kept shooting some random questions at her. Why was this untimely visit planned? If there had been some function in our hometown. When my mother tried to divert the topic, she straightaway jumped back to it."

"I heard Kashvi's marriage has been fixed. When you returned, all of us were expecting that you would be distributing sweets, hence I thought of checking with you directly."

My mother could barely respond. At that moment, I could see her face turning sad, and she was still trying to convince the lady that she had heard all the false news. I feel terrible, Sarika.

The problem is not with people being curious. The real problem is why my mother cannot share the reason behind our visit to Indore and why the marriage proposal didn't work out. Forget about my mother; why can't I share the same reason with my inquisitive colleagues in the office?

"Why is the feeling of rejection so miserable?" she questioned Sarika.

"Ignore them and don't live your life in guilt. The day you stop blaming yourself for this, you will be fine." Sarika counseled her friend.

The office hours were over.

"Leave everything aside, let us have a bike race," Sarika suggested.

"No."

"Why?" Sarika asked.

"These days, an uneasy feeling covers me, and I get nervous in a flash. Two days ago, I was returning from the market, and I experienced the same; I kept driving. After crossing 4 km, I realized I had to stop; I had missed my house lane. I will not drive until I feel better." Kashvi said in a low tone, stepping outside the office.

"Have you told Aunty about this?"

She remained quiet.

"You need to stop overthinking, as it is beginning to impact your mental health. Take this as my sincere advice, Kashvi."

"Hmm."

"You want me to drop you?" Sarika checked with her friend.

"No, I will go by autorickshaw."

At the auto stand, Kashvi saw a group of students coming out of a nearby educational institute. They all looked cheerful. Though there was no sound, she could see the noise of gestures. Looking at them, she observed that they were talking among themselves. Seeing their gestures as they expressed their feelings to their friends had slightly melted her anger. She was absorbed in their outward expressions and did not realize she was standing very close to them. Their gestures slowed down, noticing her staggered expression; a bus slowed at the stop, the group split, and they hurried to get on. The driver accelerated, and the bus disappeared.

The institute specializes in hearing and speech.

Soon, the autorickshaw arrived. 'Expression is not limited to speech. It can take many forms, including happiness, sadness, anger, laughter, tears, or even silence. She spoke to herself, experiencing an untraveled path.

When life shakes you with bitter experiences, it also reshapes you into a calmer, more mature person. Amidst all challenges, you perceive even the small conversations differently from others. That is the power of experience. The feeling of gratitude settled in her heart, easing her fury for a brief time.

Kashvi reached home and found the door was locked. She took the phone from the bag to call her mother and saw there were a few missed calls from her mother. She called her back, then heard the phone ringing somewhere nearby. She looked around and saw her mother was just a few feet away. She was carrying a bag from which green, leafy vegetables were hanging.

"You could have waited for me," she said with a sigh of tiredness.

"I waited and called, but you are always away from your phone these days," her mother complained while unlocking the door.

A few months passed, but Kashvi had not overcome the feeling of dejection. Despite keeping her engaged in various chores, the sense of desolation settled over her like a dark cloud as soon as she sat idle.

One day in the office, as the meeting ended, everyone left the meeting room, and her manager asked her to stay.

"Can you wait, Kashvi. I need to talk."

"Yes, sure." Kashvi pulled the chair back to remain seated.

"Is everything all right on your end?" he asked.

"Hmm."

"I do not like to bring this up with someone as diligent as you, but it is necessary at this point. You have been missing several deadlines, Kashvi."

"I understand. I will catch up soon," she assured.

"Do not hesitate to ask for help if you need it." He spoke before leaving the room.

She sat down to unlock her system and noticed a guy sitting adjacent to her desk was staring at her. She tried to ignore him, but his constant glare made her uncomfortable.

Every single stare was starting to disturb her. It reminded her of the meeting with Praneel's family and relatives. The stare gave a shiver to her. It triggered a fear and a shame — reminding her of that traumatic experience. She could not bear it anymore.

She could not focus on her work, and she decided to take a break. After watching her friend's sudden movement from the workstation, Sarika followed her.

"All good?" she asked Kashvi.

"I cannot keep up with this feeling anymore. I cannot tolerate this pain now. How can I get rid of it?" Kashvi asked her friend in a puzzled voice.

Sarika didn't know what to say to calm her friend down. She could see the rage in her voice that she was hiding.

"It is over," Sarika said as she peeked inside her coffee mug.

"You are right. Let us go back to work." Kashvi nodded, paying attention to her friend's hint.

While climbing the stairs of her house, she heard a carefree laughter. It was Shalini Aunty's voice.

"Here she is," Shalini Aunty spoke cheerfully, pointing at Kashvi. She was standing at the door.

"Shalini is complaining that you have not been to her house for so many days." Mrs. Sharma clarified and went inside.

Kashvi smiled in response.

"Are you going back?" Kashvi asked.

"Yes, Balraj must be angry. I have been here for the past two hours. I was waiting to meet you."

"Anything important?" Kashvi asked again.

"Nothing," she opened her arms to hug her. 'Kashvi, Praneel had called some days back. Kashvi stepped back, listening to his name to loosen the embrace. Balraj and Jiji strictly instructed me not to respond to any of his calls, but I can't hold it any longer.' She gripped her hand tightly and spoke in a hushed voice.

As Shalini Aunty noticed Mrs. Sharma approaching them. She changed the topic.

"Jiji, this Sunday, come to my place for dinner. I don't want to listen to any excuse." Saying so, she left their place.

'I am holding so much inside, and Shalini Aunty cannot keep one conversation.' Kashvi was disheartened. She wanted to free herself from this unpleasant feeling, which was difficult for her to express to anyone.

She had read somewhere that journaling your unexpressed feelings and thoughts can calm you down. Shalini Aunty's words added more sleepless nights, and she penned down:

Neither once nor twice,
I think it's infinite times, it reaches as a gush of air,
Knocking my heart and soul.
It hides somewhere in a part of the brain,
Leaving me in a forlorn way.
Making efforts to come out,
And never met this thought again;
But every time while unloading my mind,
it lurks and appears in front of my eyes.
Today it flashes again in my mind
with sudden happiness and pain,
it shuddered me in tears,
Leaving me in a forlorn way.

She found the cold and cloudy days more depressing; she longed for the bright and sunny days that made her feel a little better. As they say, "a ray of light," Kashvi felt that the ray of sunshine tremendously helped her in overcoming this somber feeling. She didn't know how long she would have to deal with this feeling. She had joined a music class to keep herself busy, engaging herself throughout the day and never allowing her mind to dwell on the past.

Apart from heartbreak, the evening when his parents came to meet her had started haunting her more. With the days passing, she was losing confidence. The stares and scornful reactions on everyone's faces were disturbing her.

"Instead of suppressing why this pain had become excruciating, she questioned herself. Was Mom right?

Should I talk to someone? Will I be able to feel normal? Can't I be happy like I used to be?" She had numerous questions on her mind.

Kashvi got a call from another company in Hyderabad, where she had applied for a job a few months ago. The recruitment panel had agreed to take an online interview, and Kashvi had cleared all the rounds.

By the end of the week, she received an offer letter. Her joining date was just a few weeks away. She had applied for this position to join a company after her marriage, when she was looking for a job in the city where Praneel lived.

"Was this change really required now?" She pondered this offer for a few days and, at last, decided to accept it. Maybe this will help me in dealing with this despair.

She informed her mother about her new job and her relocation to that city. Her mother was hesitant about her decision but agreed later as she wanted her daughter to come out of the trauma she was dealing with at that time.

The following Monday, Kashvi informed Sarika and handed in her resignation letter at the office. Days passed, tormented thoughts and sorrow had taken up permanent residence in her heart.

The only cure she could see was to change her location and meet new people.

Sarika had come to meet her before she left for Hyderabad. After a long, bittersweet talk, she slept, and Kashvi had started hating the nights for not being able to sleep, without thinking of Praneel. Don't I love my sleep now?

XIII
Harsh Reality

Kashvi had booked a flight ticket to Hyderabad; she left her place early in the morning to reach the airport on time. It was not the first time she had traveled, but she was leaving her place to relocate to a whole different city and was apprehensive about leaving her mother.

Her inquisitive mind was making it difficult for her to relax. She had several questions on her mind—had she made the right decision, or would this change help her to explore new opportunities? And the most important, will I be happy again?

With all these questions on her mind, she reached the airport almost two hours before the expected time. The cab driver helped her drop her luggage onto the trolley. She was constantly checking her luggage items. She stumbled as she was anxious and was traveling alone to an unknown city, where she hardly knew anyone.

Her college friend, with whom she is going to stay, was the only one she knew. She was sad about leaving her mother alone. She wiped that thought immediately away because if it lingered in her mind for a few more minutes, she would have canceled her plan of moving out of this city.

The entrance was crowded with people, some with happy, others with sad, goodbyes. She quickly unzipped her handbag and pulled out the ticket. In a hurry, the ID card sank into her oversized bag. She dug it out and displayed it at the entrance along with the ticket. The security guard verified it and allowed her inside. The sensor gates opened, and she felt the breeze of fresh air on her face.

Pushing her trolley, she reached the check-in counter.

"Which will move faster?" Wondering about that, she joined a queue and realized the next queue was moving faster.

"I am never good at making the right decision at the right time." She muttered in frustration.

As she leaned out of the queue to see what was going on ahead, she saw a person arguing with the airline staff about the weight of the luggage.

"Strange! What can the airline staff do if you plan to carry the entire house with you?" A sly smile appeared on her face.

Watching the argument, a young guy, who must be studying in college, stepped out of the queue. He began transferring his clothes into a small bag in a flurry. The bag, which he had kept handy to shift extra luggage.

"Wow, is he clever or careless? He knows his luggage is overweight, but he still wants to unpack and repack here, revealing his untidy clothes and innerwear." She smirked.

"How many times have I weighed my luggage after arranging a set of dresses at home?" She smiled at herself.

"Sometimes I wonder if I'm too particular about how I live or follow what I've been taught. But I don't have to be strict about every step. Letting go a little won't hurt. It can actually open up new experiences and help you enjoy life more." She realized, looking at the young guy.

Her mother had packed some snacks for her, which she had not carried, thinking what if the security staff might ask her to take them out. She did not want to add more tension when limitless, unfading worries already hemmed her in.

"I am overly cautious about many things in life. But life rarely goes as planned. No matter how much you prepare, surprises and setbacks will happen. Sometimes, the more careful you are, the more likely you are to stumble in front of others. What matters most is getting back up, not focusing on what made you fall." She said to herself.

The queue was moving slowly, and she waited for her turn. After a few minutes, she was at the counter; the air hostess asked her to keep the bag on the belt of the belt machine. Kashvi kept her fingers crossed on her left hand and passed her ID card and ticket with her right hand. Her bag weighed just 300 grams less than the recommended weight, so she simmered herself down. The air hostess allotted her the window seat, handed her the boarding pass, and informed her about the gate number.

"I was not ready to get married because I was concerned about my mother. Today, I am prepared to leave everything to regain the peace of mind I once had."

Kashvi took her boarding pass and left the trolley in the designated area, and she was soon at the security gate. In no time, she was standing on the other side of the security gate.

"Don't look back. You are on the right track." She assured herself.

She searched for Gate No. 5 and waited in the boarding area.

She looked around and found a place to sit. She found one seat next to a senior citizen. At first, she hesitated, then went to grab it as her feet were hurting badly in those heels.

"Yes, I have reached the airport safely and will soon board the flight." She called and updated her mother.

After hearing her mother's voice, the dismal feeling wrapped around her again, but she composed herself and ended the call. She took the book out of her bag and was soon lost in the new chapter. The opening line on that page read:

"People come and go from your life. Life doesn't stop for anyone. The more we stick to those memories, the more it hurts us."

Kashvi had a habit of marking the text she found meaningful in the book. In the margin of the page, she scribbled: *Papa didn't stay with us for long; After he left, Ma and I moved forward. Don't cling too much to the memories. Memories also fade over time.*

She saw people forming a queue in front of her and realized that the boarding had started. She hung her bag and kept the ticket inside the book she was holding. Soon she was on the flight and was relieved to sit in the window seat. Her hand fumbled when she fastened the seat belt; she grabbed her book tightly and closed her eyes to calm herself.

In a few minutes, she was thousands of feet above the ground. She looked out the window, and the view was stunning, with clouds that looked like cotton candy floating in the air. She looked as far as she could to see if she could see the curve of the Earth's surface.

"Perhaps life beyond this horizon would be beautiful."

She smiled at her infantile thoughts and switched back to reading.

She dozed off while reading; she woke to the captain's announcement that they would be landing in a few minutes. She found her book lying on her lap. She unfolded the papers, which were crumpled by the pressure of her hand, and kept them carefully inside her bag. The flight landed on time, and Kashvi had a hassle-free plane journey.

The city was oddly different from her hometown. She smiled when she referred to her place as her hometown for the first time in her thoughts.

"The city is the same, but I see it differently now. When I was with him, I accepted things as I received them. I look at everything a little more carefully now. I am not as simple and naïve as I used to be." She took a deep breath, speaking to herself.

There was so much traffic on the road that she had hardly covered 8 km after getting into the city from the airport road. Everybody was honking and in a hurry. Strange faces, unfriendly expressions, skyscraping buildings, crowded lanes, colorful taxis, brand shops, malls, and the traffic lights, which hardly work in her hometown, and a few trees on the roadside. Didn't I notice all this in my last visit? she questioned in the back of her mind and quickly shut herself again.

She felt she had inhaled enough carbon dioxide in those minutes. She wanted to close the window, but the driver had mentioned that the AC was not working. She had kept the window shades down to keep herself away from getting suffocated. It took 2.5 hours to reach her friend's place from the city's airport.

Meera was delighted to meet Kashvi and immediately hugged her. Kashvi, as always reserved with her response and gesture, pretended to hug her, but she was happy to meet Meera, too. She dragged one of Kashvi's suitcases and asked whether her commute from the airport to her place was easy. Kashvi smiled and said it was an easy, long drive.

"I am so happy that you shifted here. I miss my friends. I have found so many friends here, but you know the real friends are from college, not from the office," said Meera and winked at her.

Kashvi smiled and agreed. They entered the lift and reached the ninth floor. She helped Kashvi pull the luggage out and unlocked the door. It was a one-bedroom flat, but spacious. Kashvi found it small because she had never lived in an apartment, but she knew this was the best she could afford, given her new job in the city. There was a long, spacious balcony from where she could see only concrete buildings, which, according to Meera, was the best view of all the flats she had lived in this city so far.

Meera showed her the bedroom, and as only two of them are living in that apartment, she could choose to sleep in the hall. There were two cupboards in the bedroom; out of the two, one was already empty, or maybe Meera would have cleared it for Kashvi to keep her stuff.

She told her about the domestic helper who comes to clean and mop, but in the evening, they have to clean the utensils themselves.

"If you want, you can join the canteen nearby, or you can also choose to have a tiffin service, pretend having homemade food alone from the box sitting here," added Meera and laughed.

"How do you manage?" Kashvi asked hesitantly.

"Oh, I love cooking, so I cook by myself," she cheerfully answered.

"Amazing!" Kashvi replied.

"If you want, then we can both buy and divide the grocery bills," said Meera.

"Yes, that should be fine," answered Kashvi.

"Great, do you like cooking, or would you like to wash utensils?" she asked, followed by a laugh.

"Ah, anything is fine with me, until you do any experiment with the food," Kashvi timidly replied.

She took a shower and realized she had to call her mother now. She informed her that she had reached Meera's place and would be joining her office from tomorrow.

"Take care and don't stress yourself," her mother advised.

Meera had already set the dinner on the table. They both sat down to eat. She asked her about her office location. Kashvi mentioned the name of the tech park where the company was located.

"Oh, it is almost 20 km from here," Meera replied.

"You need to change multiple buses as there is no direct transport from here. And if you are ready to burn your money on these cabs, you can take a cab and go directly to your office."

"Certainly not," shook Kashvi.

"Then, you take a bus from here to Big City Mall, and from there, you need to walk for almost 500-800 meters, and then take another bus to your office. If you don't get the direct bus from there, don't keep waiting for that bus; take any bus that drops you on the way to your office. Otherwise, the whole day you will be waiting at the stop. You can also take an auto in between if they agree to go by meter, or see if any shared autos or cabs are available. Anyway, in a week, you will get used to it and will know many better options to commute faster and easier," Meera suggested.

Kashvi was overwhelmed by the information but digested it along with dinner.

They cleared their plates, and Kashvi helped her clean the dishes and the kitchen.

"Would you like to use the bedroom? I am fine to sleep in the living room." Meera asked generously.

Kashvi was already guilty of taking her space and helping her so much in the new city, so she replied, "No, I can use the hall."

Kashvi was tired of all the information she had received from Meera and was nervous about whether she would be able to cope in this city. She was already feeling homesick. She did not get a sound sleep and was disrupted multiple times by her pensive mood.

The alarm rang at 6 AM, and she woke up without snoozing it off. She looked around the apartment and missed her mother's morning prayer. She was ready by 7 AM and went into the kitchen to make some breakfast. She found a packet of bread and butter lying in the refrigerator. She prepared a sandwich for herself and then realized she should also make one for Meera.

While keeping all the necessary documents for her first day, she missed her morning tea with her mother.

It was 8 o'clock, so she left for her office.

She followed every instruction given by Meera and had successfully reached halfway to her office. She managed to get a seat on the bus but could not get the change back from the conductor, which was about 8 rupees. She was in a dilemma whether to take the chance or give up, and at last sacrificed her money.

Her mind began calculating how much she would lose in a month if this happened at least twice a day, waiting for the bus at the next stop. Luckily, she got the direct bus to her office from this stop. She boarded the bus, and the ticket fare was Rs 14. She was missing her piggy bank at home, and with a heavy heart, she took out a 100 Rupee note. While she was calculating how much she would lose if she didn't get the change back, the conductor gave her a nasty look upon seeing the 100 Rupee note in her hand.

"Can't you keep change handy?" he asked rudely.

"Where will I get change, especially early in the morning?" she wanted to say, but she couldn't and showed her purse to him. Kashvi, totally oblivious to the situation, was embarrassed and wanted to get off at the next stop, but her office was still far away. Finally, she reached her office and even got the change back.

She got down, fixed her hair and dress before entering the tech park. It was a huge space with multiple tall buildings on the premises. She entered the office and felt relieved upon reaching the reception counter.

One by one, the new employees began to fill the training room. The room was buzzing with murmurs, whispers, and hushed laughter. Most of them looked excited and curious, holding coffee cups, staring at the screen, and waiting for the session to start. At the end of the training, a chorus of voices hummed to get answers. Among them, Kashvi also blurted out her question. The heads turned to look back as she was sitting in the last row, but she felt everybody was staring at her intently, which was certainly not the case.

"The glare, as always, reminds me of the meeting. I need to learn to ignore the stare." She muttered.

However, the silence in the room made her uncomfortable. Her hand trembled with fear, and she struggled to speak.

To steady her composure, she silently held a cup on the table and voiced her question. The training was over, and Kashvi waited for the crowd to disperse. Staring at the screen, she wished she could ever trust herself again. Her hands were still cold from the unintentional, sudden shock she experienced in the room. She had lost her confidence.

Some experiences haunt you forever. No matter how much you try to get rid of it.

After her office hour, she followed the same route and reached home on time. She called her mother and spoke about everything—the city, office, team members, Meera, and most importantly, her daily commute to her office.

It was a busy week for Kashvi, and she did not realize how quickly time flew by. One weekend, Meera had gone on an office trip, leaving Kashvi bored with her usual routine. She was looking at her phone, scrolling through messages. Suddenly, her phone rang, the same number flashed on the screen, and she trembled as she answered.

Hi, Kashvi, he said in a dull voice.

It had been more than six months since he had heard her voice. He experienced a sudden relief listening to her.

'I had called you a couple of times.' With a brief pause, he said, 'You didn't reply to my messages. I had called Sarika, and she informed me about your relocation. You didn't even inform me that you have shifted to Hyderabad." He asked in an authoritative tone.

"Was it even required?" She snapped.

In a flash, he realized he did not have the right to ask such a question.

"Can we meet, Kashvi?"

She did not answer and disconnected the call.

Gloominess has once again besieged her. The sorrow she was hiding from everyone for so long has crept in again. Nothing has changed. It weighs the same. It is as heavy as the day everything broke.

"Am I fooling myself by running away from my grief?"

"For a week, I didn't even think much about him, but this call had scratched my wounds again. I don't have my mom or Sarika to console me here." She hated herself for picking up the call. She kept thinking about everything all night and couldn't sleep that night again.

She spent her weekend keeping herself busy by reading and exploring the places in her local area.

A few months have passed, and Kashvi has made a few friends in this city now. Although she kept herself busy with something at all times, she was unable to get rid of her memories of Praneel.

One day, when she was having lunch, she got a call from Praneel. She hesitated but picked up the call again.

"Hello, Kashvi!

"Why have you called?"

"Can we meet?" He asked again. She paused, agreed to the meeting.

Kashvi couldn't concentrate on her work that day. She was puzzled, thinking whether she had done the right thing by agreeing to meet Praneel. She wanted to leave the office early, but there were a few deadlines, so she had to stay late to complete her work. She reached home late.

On the way, she saw there was a message from Praneel. He had mentioned the time and place where he would be waiting for Kashvi tomorrow.

She reached home and checked with Meera how far that location is from their apartment. That whole night, she couldn't sleep, doubting her decision. She kept tossing and turning on her bed. She kept forcing herself to fall asleep, but she couldn't sleep peacefully.

"There are only two things in my life. Either I want to sleep, or I want to read. How much can I keep myself occupied to forget the bitter experience I went through that day?" She tried to wipe all memories of that meeting, but it was not easy. Around 3 AM, she fell asleep.

Her alarm rang at 6:00 AM. While getting ready, she had a train of thought: "Why am I meeting him? Should I go or cancel the plan? Shall I tell Mom or Sarika? What am I going to talk about?"

She was bemused and then decided to meet him. She checked her bag to see if there was sufficient change to buy tickets, and her mobile was charged enough to survive a little longer.

Praneel had already reached the meeting spot. The wait seemed long, and with every passing minute, he anxiously looked at the bus stop, hoping to see her. At last, he parked his car and called her. When the bus stopped, and she got off, she found Praneel standing just a few steps away from the stop.

He smiled, looking at Kashvi. The smile was dull, not the same as what she had seen on his face when they had met. When Praneel looked at her, he found her eyes were still captivating but lacked the spark this time.

When they looked at each other, neither were they happy nor sad, but still greeted each other with a smile. They did not know why they experienced such indifferent emotions nowadays.

"How far is the restaurant from here?" she asked.

"Not too far, it is a 30-minute drive from here," he replied.

"I have parked the car a little far from here." They both walked for a few meters and reached the parking spot. After sitting inside, they both ignored each other's glances to hide their feelings. Kashvi felt the drive was slow and asked if there was something wrong with his car. He ignored her question.

He could have driven at a reasonable pace, but he wanted to spend time with Kashvi as much as he could. He kept asking her about her new job and company. Kashvi did not ask any questions and kept replying to his questions. They soon reached the well-known restaurant where Praneel had already reserved a table for them, so without much wait, they got a seat. Praneel took the menu and started turning the pages to see the available lunch options. In the meantime, she got a call from her mother.

"Hello," she answered the call.

"Where are you? It is the weekend, and you usually call in the morning. I was worried if everything is fine with you." Mrs. Sharma asked in a concerned voice.

"I have come outside to meet someone."

"Who?"

"Praneel." She informed her mother.

Praneel heard her response, but he pretended to check the listed items on the menu and continued staring at her from the corner of his eye. He knew her extremely well and was aware that she would have either informed her mother or would inform her now, which she did.

He knew that Kashvi talks less and is bad at giving diplomatic answers. She is modest when talking to people, but she surprises them by giving sudden, blunt replies.

"What, but, why? And you did not inform me." Mrs. Sharma voiced her concerns by asking questions.

"Am I not informing you now?" she replied, justifying her answer.

"You are impossible," said Mrs. Sharma with disapproval.

"I will talk to you when I reach home," Kashvi said, and then disconnected the call.

She found Praneel staring at her, which made her feel awkward. Kashvi kept her phone in her bag and tried not to look at Praneel.

"Have you informed your parents?" She asked, filling in the silence.

"What...that I am going to meet you?" he asked and smiled." Kashvi felt stupid for asking such a question.

"What would you like to have?" he asked. She looked slightly abashed for not getting the answer to her other question.

Praneel caught sight of it and answered.

'After a point, you don't need to tell everything to everyone. I feel I don't owe anyone an explanation unless I do something wrong. Do we?' he asked Kashvi in his deep voice.

"Parents don't belong to the 'Anyone' category," she replied.

Praneel noticed the waiter standing closer to her, ready to pen down the order in his notepad. With his glare, he just shifted a few steps away and asked, "What would you like to have?"

They ordered food, and Kashvi asked him to add juice to their order. The waiter took the order, and due to the rush during lunch hours, informed them that it would take a few extra minutes than usual and moved to another table.

He knew Kashvi wouldn't talk much, so to fill in the awkward silence, Praneel kept asking her about her plans, her aunt and uncle, whom he met in Gwalior. He asked about her mom.

Because Praneel had asked her about her mother, she felt the need to ask about his parents out of courtesy.

"How are uncle and aunty?" she asked in a low voice.

Lunch arrived, and the waiter started serving the food on their plates. He placed the juice glass near Kashvi. Praneel ignored her question and started eating his food. After a gulp of juice, she repeated her question.

"How are aunty and uncle?"

He looked up and took the glass from Kashvi's hand, wearing a grim smile on his face.

"I don't know," he answered.

She was startled by his gesture. His fingers touched her hand, and she quivered.

She waited for him to complete his sentence. After months of talking on the call, they were both so familiar with each other's behavior that they could interpret each other's responses and anticipate their next move.

He took a sip from the same glass and continued.

"I don't know because it has been a long time since I called them." He spoke, looking closely into her eyes.

She saw his face had turned red. She jiggled a little, which he had noticed, and was very well aware that angry reactions upset her. He remembered Kashvi telling him once that she becomes uncomfortable seeing angry faces around her and prefers to be with placid people.

He calmed himself, and he offered the same glass, without thinking. She didn't drink the juice from that glass again.

He kept waiting for her to say something about what happened in Indore when she met his parents, but she did not bring it up in any of their discussions.

He felt the weight of unsaid words and broke the silence.

"I tried." He spoke in a hushed voice. His hands reached for her hands, resting on the table.

She quickly moved her hands away before he could hold them. He smiled at her gesture. His smile still carried the same affection for her.

"You are fortunate to have a mother like Aunty." He added.

'I will take a leave now.' She informed, looking at her watch.

He was not prepared for this response and wanted to stop her from spending some more time with her, but he lacked the courage.

He inquired about her address, but she did not answer and waved at the autorickshaw parked a few feet away.

The autorickshaw approached and stopped next to them.

"I could have dropped you," she ignored and quickly sat inside, smiling at him.

'See you.'

'Goodbye,' she replied, and the autorickshaw left.

Parting from loved ones is never easy. It takes courage to leave someone or to be with someone.

Some people neither leave you nor hold you back, leaving your life stuck at a standstill. This is the time to decide and let go. The talks, the complaints, the expectations, the anger, the grief—all remained unexpressed. The hidden desire to pour all her feelings out in front of him had faded, and silence settled deep inside her heart.

Somewhere deep inside her heart, she wanted to ask, 'Why can't you convince your parents? If you were so weak, why did you make all those promises? Why have you put me in this terrible situation? All of you took charge of my life and decided everything, leaving me in this situation that I don't deserve.'

"Or do I deserve it? I always questioned my friends, how can they date someone, love someone, and spend life with another person? Is this the reason I am in this situation now?"

*"Was this Murphy's law? I was focused on the negative side from day one. I was afraid of **heartbreak without falling in love.**"*

"Or is this the universe's way of telling me not to make too many rules in life? You don't have control over it."

Learn, smile, and move on with courage; life has better plans for you.

Consoling herself, she reached home feeling dejected. The sound of the doorbell brought her attention back to the real world, prompting her to set her inner talks aside.

She pulled her lips to the corner of her mouth to smile back at Meera as she opened the gate, smiling at her.

"Hey, Kashvi, sorry I couldn't wake up on time. How was your meeting with your friend?"

"It was good," she answered, keeping her bag on the table. She went straight to the bathroom. Wearing a polite smile, she stared in the mirror. Slowly, lifted her hand and turned it upside down, gently traced her fingers on her cheeks, and recalled the remark made by Mrs. Tripathi.

There were so many advocates in the courtyard that evening. Everybody gathered to hear the judge's verdict. Your values do not matter; your skin color matters.

She was shattered by his mother's remark. The only thing that lingered in her mind was her sharp words. She had started seeing herself through the harsh words of Mrs. Tripathi.

"When will this leave me?" She questioned herself.

She pulled her lips a little wider; the smile was carrying the pain.

When she came out, Meera had kept the tea ready for her on the table. She mentioned that she was going to a party and would return home late.

"No need to wait for me. Have your dinner and sleep," suggested Meera.

Kashvi quietly listened to whatever she said and nodded in agreement. Meera had left for the party, and Kashvi was alone in the house, which she hated. The loneliness was troubling her, and she wanted to talk to her mother.

When you are alone, you are left with thoughts. The string of never-ending, troubling questions that keep getting weirder and longer. At the end, you are left with the cruel answer that you are trying to escape.

She called her mother.

"Hello Kashvi, why has that guy come to meet you, and why did you agree to meet?" Mrs. Sharma sounded angry.

"I wanted to meet him," she replied in a dull tone.

Her mother was silent, knowing her daughter was not all right.

"Are you fine, Kashvi?"

"Yes," she said, trying to sound brave. "I will come back home tomorrow.

Her mother understood her daughter's state of mind and asked her to relax and not to think too much.

Kashvi booked her return ticket. She sent an email to the office saying she is not well and will be on leave for a few weeks. She didn't care whether it got approved or if she would be fired, as she had hardly completed a few months in that company. She wanted to return home.

Her phone rang again. His name flashed again on the screen. Like always, she picked up the call again.

Did you reach home safely?

'Yes,' she replied.

'I have been worried.'

She didn't reply.

'Are you okay, Kashvi? You have every right to complain and be angry with me, but don't hate me," Praneel spoke in a disheartened voice. She disconnected the call.

The uneasy feeling was troubling her, so she engaged herself in packing her luggage and set it in a corner of the room to avoid blocking the hallway. To her surprise, Meera returned from the party before time.

"Are you going somewhere?" she asked, looking at her luggage.

"Yes," Kashvi said quietly.

"Hope everything is fine at your end," Meera inquired.

"Yes, I am feeling homesick. I want to meet my mother. I will leave early tomorrow morning. I have done the calculation and have transferred my share, along with this month's rent," Kashvi added.

'Are you not returning, Kashvi?' Meera asked.

'I am not sure,' Kashvi replied.

The very next morning, the airport taxi arrived at the apartment gate by 4:30 AM. She smiled and bid adieu to Meera.

By 2 PM, she was in Gwalior. When Kashvi stepped down from the taxi, she smiled and looked at her house. Her mother was standing on the balcony facing toward the road, waiting for her daughter.

Home heals every pain. You cannot keep yourself away from it for long. The run always ends at home.

Mrs. Sharma helped her keep her things in her room. She was feeling better now. Her heartbeat was normal compared to last night.

"Change your clothes, Kashvi. Lunch is ready. Let us have it together."

After changing her dress, she went inside and checked the serving bowls. Mrs. Sharma had prepared all her daughter's favorite food; the delicious aroma unblocked her senses, which she felt had been blocked by pollution in the big city.

They both quietly had their lunch. Kashvi was exhausted and went to sleep in her room. Mrs. Sharma went inside to see Kashvi and noticed she was in a deep sleep. She called and informed Sarika about Kashvi's return.

In the evening, she was happy to see Sarika at her home. Kashvi knew that her mom was angry about her meeting with Praneel, but she had not questioned her until now.

Sarika shared everything that happened in her absence and how much she missed her dear friend, while Kashvi listened quietly.

They had dinner, and while they were all talking, Sarika and her mother noticed that Kashvi was still quiet and once again lost in thought.

"Are you fine?" Sarika inquired.

Her eyes were welling up with tears. As Sarika placed her hand on her shoulder, tears rolled down her cheeks and flowed continuously. Though she wanted to stop crying, she couldn't control her tears. She kept wiping her tears, but they kept flowing.

"Why did you meet that guy?" Mrs. Sharma asked.

"You were fine until now. Who suggested you meet him?" she questioned again.

"It all ended with that meeting, so why are you still connected with him? Is he calling you?" her mother was asking a series of questions.

"No," she interjected. I wanted to meet him. I wanted to meet one last time. I wanted to see how a person who talks so much about love and affection can forget everything so easily. I wanted to ask, if he did not dare to make his parents understand his choices, why had he made those promises to me?"

"Have you asked?" Sarika inquired quietly.

"No," she replied, wiping her tears. There was silence in the room for a while.

"It feels impossible for now, but I know that as the days pass, I will be fine. I will forget him someday.

There is no such thing as 'going with the flow'. If you feel something is not right, bring it up and get it resolved immediately rather than waiting and facing something worse. It happened to me because I agreed to that proposal, as you all felt it was right. I only questioned about the meeting with his parents, but I never took the right step to stop it at the right time. It is nobody's mistake, but it is my mistake. It happens when we leave the major decision of our life in somebody else's hands, and I learned it from a bitter experience in my life."

"And I don't want to marry anyone, stop looking for it," she said, looking at her mother. Her eyes were still filled with tears, yet she carried a stern expression.

"I am tired of this continuous run now."

With a broken heart, the love was lost, and a confident, vital piece of herself, too.

Kashvi went into her room to sleep, leaving Sarika and her mother in the room.

The room was filled with heavy and aching silence.

'It was my fault. If I had not agreed to her uncle's proposal of meeting this guy, she would have never gone through this pain.' Mrs. Sharma spoke in a dull voice.

'Do you know Sarika? In my college days, I had many friends who were beautiful and intelligent, but none of our parents asked us about our choice when our marriages were fixed. Whether we liked the person or not, nobody bothered. In fact, we all got married, and some of us went against our wishes.'

"Arranging and fixing a daughter's marriage is more important than anything else in our society. We encourage them to become independent, but never give them real freedom. I did the same. Had it been Praneel, not Kashvi, would this question have ever arisen? Would I have denied this proposal, saying, 'No, your son's complexion doesn't match my daughter's?'

For Kashvi, it was her complexion, and for others, it must be their weight, height, and features. We judge people based on their appearance. We don't even realize how these demeaning reactions and comments can affect a person's life. How does it affect their confidence? How much does it emotionally damage them? How much does it harm a person's mental well-being?"

"The worst thing we can ever do is to make someone feel inferior and forget that God has created everyone, and we are showing our disapproval of His creativity."

Watch your words and actions, and be kind to people.

It takes years to overcome these feelings, but they remain with a person for a lifetime. They cannot even share it with someone because they feel ridiculed again by talking about themselves. We won't understand it until we experience it. The kind of turmoil a person goes through is unthinkable.

His parents and relatives did not say anything to Kashvi that evening, but their disapproval, merely by looking at her, had affected her self-esteem.

We cannot control the third person's behavior, but we can teach our children to set up boundaries before somebody crosses their line to hurt them, which I failed to do.

After a long and insightful discussion with her mother, Sarika also went into the room to sleep.

'In the country of Goddess Kali and Lord Krishna, we are obsessed with fair complexion,' Mrs. Sharma uttered. She picked up Kashvi's phone, deleted Praneel's messages and number from her contact list.

Life unwraps several pleasant and unpleasant surprises at different stages of life. On the day when differences and disagreements arise, the promises, planning, affirmation, and commitment lose their essence.

Were they destined to split up?

In many regions of India, anything that is 'dark', or I should rather say 'black',is considered undesirable. In some regions, people even discourage their children from drinking tea, fearing it might darken their skin. It sounds quirky, but it is an unpleasant fact. An average-looking individual often faces challenges in the entertainment industry and struggles to become a leading figure. In schools, it has been observed many times that thin, ordinary-looking children are not chosen to stand in the front row during events and functions.

The obsession with having a light skin tone was always there, or is it something we were influenced by during British colonialism? The media also promotes skin-lightening products and admires fair-skinned individuals over those with darker complexions.

Society frequently associates good looks and physical appearance with social and economic status. When people face this bias, especially from childhood, they may dislike themselves for their physical appearance. Because they compare themselves with others on the so-called good looks parameter, they always live under the fear of rejection.

From an early age, they feel unworthy and lack the confidence to attain certain positions or roles in the workplace. They struggle with self-esteem from a young age, feeling overshadowed by others.

Above all else, there is a custom in arranged marriage proposals where the "Groom-to-be's" family often visits to meet the "Bride-to-be's" family. To put it plainly, the sole purpose of such meetings is— to see "what the girl looks like?" Is she beautiful? Strangely, in this case, the beauty doesn't lie in the eyes of the beholder; it lies in their physical appearance.

Settled in the Silicon Valley of India, I thought the custom of scrutinizing girls based on their looks no longer exists. However, I was wrong. Hearing experiences from some girls about how they had been asked to march in front of the groom's family was tormenting. The match-making meeting—to match the height, weight, and color— still exists.

The most awful thing I heard— when a girl was asked to show her feet so the groom's family could be assured that the skin tone of her feet matches her face. All these incidents sound dramatic when we hear or read in articles, but that is the truth of our society.

It is easy to comment on someone's physical appearance. Whether it is skin tone, height, or weight, it might not seem like a serious issue until you are rebuffed. It can severely impact an individual's confidence and mental health. It can even cause trauma, which, as a society, we often fail to notice.

Nothing wrong in dreaming of a beautiful partner, but don't mistreat anyone only because they don't weigh appropriately on your "good-looks" parameter.

No one deserves to be mistreated.